BEASTLY CROWN

A BEAUTY AND THE BEAST ROMANTASY

THE LUNATERRA CHRONICLES
BOOK ONE

INES JOHNSON

PROLOGUE

ADOM

My first memory was of screaming. Shrill, gut-wrenching screams, sharp enough to pierce the veil of unconsciousness. It was a sound I had no name for then but would come to know well—fear. The kind of fear that clawed its way through the air and lodged itself in the bones.

They weren't my screams. Later I would wonder if they should have been.

The screaming belonged to the midwife. She stumbled from the chamber, pale and wide-eyed, clutching her skirts as though something unspeakable was chasing her. I wasn't chasing her. I was too busy taking my first breath in this world.

Breathing came as naturally to me as seeing clearly in the darkened room. Seeing and discerning figures came as naturally as turning over onto my belly and coming to my paws to stand. I also knew that if I opened my tiny paws, the sharp claws would draw blood.

The air in the room was thick with the earthy tang of blood and the faint, coppery scent of sweat. Inhaling the second breath of my life, I decided I liked them both.

A set of massive hands came toward me. They were unclawed. Bigger than my entire person. My tiny heart pounded as the giant brought my body to him. When he spoke, my fear dissipated. He was not going to eat me.

I'd heard my father's voice every day of my existence in the womb. His booming laugh when he spoke with his friends. The different voices he used as he read me stories of daring princes, beautiful damsels, and evil villains. The amorous whispers he spoke in private to my mother. The guttural cries when he was training with his warriors.

He gathered me in his arms and held me against the strong beat of his chest, grinning proudly as though I were something precious. His callused fingers were gentle against my skin, like he was trying to comfort me. Realization dawned that something was wrong. With me.

My father bent down and placed me in her arms. Her body trembled as she took me. Not the shivering cold of someone afraid for their life. Her lips quivered, her golden eyes—so sharp, so striking—filled with unshed tears. Not a single one fell. It was my first lesson as her son.

My mother looked at me like I wasn't whole. Like she couldn't decide whether to toss me from her or clutch me closer. I caught my reflection in the flash of her cat-gold irises. If I were her, I would've chosen to cry out and toss me away.

I didn't need a mirror to tell me that the sight of me would turn stomachs or send maids screaming from the room. I could feel it in the way my body didn't feel like a body at all. Not fully boy. Not fully beast. A liminal thing, caught between worlds.

Mother blinked, and the reflection was gone. She pulled me to her chest. Her heartbeat thundered against my ears. I was hers—a lioness's cub. Her trembling arms said what her words couldn't: She would protect me.

I belonged to her. Just like my father did. She would protect us both.

I was only ten solars old when that protection broke.

The day my father died in the Troll Wars, the world I knew crumbled. Grief swept through the palace like a storm. It didn't roar or howl as it left destruction in its wake. It didn't come in sobs or wails—it settled in the walls, in the air, in the spaces between us, dismantling what was left of our family with devastating quiet.

The queen's silence was a heavy, unyielding thing that pressed against my chest like a stone. She shut herself away from the world. In the hollow space she left behind, I heard what she didn't say aloud.

I felt it in every wincing glance she sent my way in the darkness of her rooms. I saw it in every averted gaze at the dinner table. The curse that marked me was a symbol of the forbidden path my parents had chosen. Their love, a defiance against the will of a god, had brought ruin. Avarix had punished them, not with fire or famine, but with me.

I was their mistake. A reminder of their rebellion, their hubris. An abomination born of a love that never should have been.

I grew into that beast. My body followed the curse, growing monstrously larger, fiercer. My mane thickened, my claws sharpened, and my roar carried across battlefields, terrifying enemies and allies alike.

On Lunaterra, a boy became a man after the planet

made thirteen revolutions around the Mother Sun and the Daughter Sun. Parties were thrown for a man child in honor of the thirteen moons that chased the Daughter Sun across the night sky hoping for her favor. There was no party thrown for me on my thirteenth solar. Only a cheer sent up across the battlefield after I made my first kill on that night.

In the land of Solmane, the center of Lunaterra, people whispered of the Beast Prince. Fear was a shield, stronger than their pity. It was easier to embody the monster they believed I was than to show the boy who still longed for something as impossible as his mother's love in the light of his father's death.

Each battle I fought brought more victories. With every drop of blood I spilled, my mother slowly began to emerge from the shadowed confines of her grief. She spoke some. She moved through the halls a bit. She even glanced at me a time or two during battle briefings. But even as her silence lifted, the threat of the trolls only deepened. Without Avarix's protection, the trolls' numbers swelled unchecked, their attacks growing bolder and bloodier and ever closer to the capitol city of Pridehaven.

There was only one way to stop the senseless war. Only one path to salvation for my people. Only one way to break the curse that kept me chained between man and beast.

I would have to do what my parents had refused.

I would marry the girl the First Moon had chosen. The one Avarix decreed would restore balance. Not the girl I had loved.

There was no girl I loved. Because no girl would ever love me. Damsels, fairy princesses, and girls lost in the forest never fell for the brutish beasts.

I buried any fairytale notions deep within me, locked away with the part of me that still remembered the softness of my father's calluses, the hope in his smile, and the love he shared with me and my mother.

All that remained was the beast. And beasts did not need love.

CHAPTER ONE

BELLE

The carriage lurched again, jostling me against the hard, embroidered seat. I clenched the fabric of the wedding gown tighter in my hands. I smoothed over a small wrinkle that hadn't been there a moment ago. The golden silk shimmered in the sunlight filtering through the carriage windows. The threads of embroidery glistened like citrine spun by a crystal scarab. It was perfect.

I had made sure of that. I showed off my gods-given talent in every stitch. Every bead was a testament to my skill, to the hours I had spent hunched over my creation, my hands cramping but my heart full of determination. This gown was more than an offering. It was my chance to be seen.

Except it was missing something.

More beading on the bodice? No, that would weigh on the bustline and give the Solmane elite a show they weren't paying for.

A longer train, more dramatic and sweeping? No, that would distract from the intricate details of the embroidery.

Another bump in the road sent the dress shifting. The uneven path on the road to Solmane threatened to undo everything I'd worked for. I clutched the bodice to my chest, then raised my knees where the gown draped down to ensure the train wouldn't touch the carriage floor.

"We could've taken the portal, Mother. It would've been faster."

"We are not peasants, Charlotte. We are royalty. We have no need for speed."

The air in the carriage was heavy with the sweetness of lilac, a cloying scent radiating from the Fairy Queen across from me. Her skin, pale as a lily's petal, glowed faintly in the shadowed interior. She sat with perfect poise, her hands folded primly in her lap. The hyacinth blood in her veins made her appear regal, cool, and untouchable.

"We could let the pegasuses fly instead of walking on land like common steeds."

"If we flew, then we would not be seen."

"That makes no sense. We don't want to appear like peasants, but we want them to see us."

"Exactly. We are to be seen and heard, like any good little princess."

Seated next to me, Princess Charlotte slouched against the velvet cushions. Her blue eyes, sharp as shards of glass, gazed out the window in abject boredom and irritation. Her posture was a deliberate rebellion, her mud-caked boots propped casually out in front of her, almost touching her mother's pristine white gown. Her lavender skin was the same shade as mine, yet it seemed softer, somehow more delicate, as though the Verbena blood from her father gave her a kind of ethereal fragility I lacked. We even had the same hair color, a dark purple that was almost black. But her hair was a wild tangle of dark curls, framing her face like a halo of defiance.

She noticed me staring and smirked, dragging her boot across the carriage floor, leaving a faint smear of dirt. Her blue eyes caught on her wedding gown in my lap. "Relax, Belle. The Beast Prince won't care if there's a wrinkle in the gown. He'll be too busy ripping it off me on our wedding night."

"Enough, Charlotte." Queen Indira snapped her lily-white fingers in a controlled gesture of disapproval. "You have been training for this since the day you were born."

"You know who else trains since the day they're born? Warriors in the Convergence Games. Except if they don't pass muster, they die. Lucky bastards."

"Watch your language. Your death would inconvenience both the Queen Lioness and the First Moon. Would you be so selfish?"

Charlotte's brows lifted as though she was debating it.

I fought to keep both my face and her wedding gown straight. I needed her to be the opposite of selfish. I needed her to put on this dress in two days' time and get married in front of all the Houses of Lunaterra so that I could become the most sought-after dressmaker on the planet.

The wheels hit another rut, jarring us sharply. The tension inside the carriage snapped, fast and merciless, like the jaws of a Venus flytrap closing around an unsuspecting insect, its teeth locking shut with a finality that left no room for escape. Lucky bug.

I did agree with Charlotte on the mode of transportation. If Queen Indira would have just let the pegasuses unfurl their powerful wings and take to the sky, we'd be in the capital city already.

Since I was a common peasant, I didn't voice my

opinion because I understood exactly what the queen was doing. This journey, like the wedding spectacle, was all about being seen. The Fairy Queen wanted all to see their wealth. Problem was, the coffers back home in Evergrove weren't dwindling; they were empty. I knew that because I had worked in a few high fae houses as a young sprout. Bank ledgers could lie, but the cutlery never did.

Most faekind were not fans of iron. To some it was an irritant, to others, it was lethal. In high fae houses that were falling on hard times, sterling silver would quietly give way to polished steel, then to tin, and finally to nothing at all. By the time I arrived at the Fairy Queen's house two years ago, there wasn't even a full set of any dishware left.

The fields outside the window blurred past. The vibrant greens and golds of the countryside glowed under the light of the two suns. The larger mother sun, Solara, cast her soft yellow light over everything. Lyra, the smaller sun, danced around her mother's halo, shining her red aura bright enough that even a fairy didn't dare look directly at her rays. Somewhere in that distant glow, the capital city of Pridehaven loomed.

"Charlotte, fix your dress. Your wings are showing. Do you want Her Lioness to think you're some flaming Ember Fae?"

Charlotte rolled her eyes again in a very unprincess-like manner. She straightened, taking care to tuck the tip of her purple wing back into her dress. Her blue gaze flicked to me, and she rolled her eyes in the opposite direction in a bid for female solidarity.

I looked down at the wedding gown. I couldn't afford to side with her. I had to agree with her mother if I wanted the fairy princess in my creation, walking down that aisle for all to see. I couldn't even sympathize about the groom. He was a prince, for suns' sake.

Sure, he was called the Beast Prince. Sure, there were rumors of women fainting at the sight of him. I had never seen him myself. There were no images captured of his actual likeness in the fashion and gossip zines. Just monstrous caricatures of a snaggle-toothed, dark-horned, furry creature.

He'd been betrothed to the fairy princess since her birth, but he'd never once set foot in Evergrove to show himself. I wasn't sure if that was a kind mercy to Charlotte or an omen of what was to come. Most royal portraits in the history books did not depict attractive faces. How could they, with all the inbreeding over the centuries? At least the royals of Solmane were reaching across the vines for a Faekind.

The carriage came to an abrupt halt, jolting me forward and pulling me from my thoughts. Outside, the muffled sounds of guards moving into position broke the stillness, their boots crunching against the gravel.

The door swung open, letting in a burst of sunlight. A thin man with a sharp, angular face stepped forward and bowed deeply.

"Greetings, Your Royal Highnesses. I am Colson, chamberlain of Pridehaven Palace. Prince Adom has charged me with escorting you to the Summer Castle."

"The Summer Castle? We were told to arrive at Pridehaven Palace."

"Yes, Highness. However, the prince is waiting inside the Summer Castle, which is just down this road. He wishes to greet his bride in private before entering the palace grounds."

In the distance, a dull white castle loomed. The walls surrounding the structure were cracked and weathered, streaked with the stains of time and neglect. Ivy crept unchecked over the battlements, its green tendrils a contrast against the lifeless stone. The windows, framed in faded arches, appeared dark and vacant, like empty eyes gazing over the surrounding landscape. The castle lacked the splendor of royalty, its tired façade speaking of years without care or use.

The Fairy Queen turned sharply to Colson, her lips pressed into a thin, unamused line. "Princess Charlotte would be delighted to have a rendezvous with her betrothed."

A flash of fear crossed Charlotte's face, quick as lightning but unmistakable. Instinctively, I reached for her hand, hoping to offer her some reassurance. Her fingers met mine in a grip so tight it sent a jolt through my arm. She might be a delicate princess, but she was strong. Hopefully, that would serve her in her new life as queen.

Colson gave a polite bow. The door to the carriage shut, and we were moving again. The moment we were out of hearing distance from the chamberlain, the queen turned to me and hissed, "Fix her. Now."

I untangled my fingers from Charlotte's and did what I was told. My hands went first to Charlotte's boots. The mud moved away from the leather of her shoes and slipped between the cracks of the carriage door.

Next was her dress. With a rotation of my wrist, I pulled the dirt from the hem of her sullied dress. The brown spots did as I bade them and dissipated into the air.

Her hair was going to be a challenge. I cracked my knuckles in a very unladylike gesture before flexing my fingers. Her tangled curls fought back, but they were no match for my magic. By the time the carriage pulled up to the white castle, Princess Charlotte was in presentable form.

The queen didn't even offer a thank you. She nodded at me like my magic was her due. In a way, it was. One solar ago, she'd caught me helping Charlotte clean off dirt from a gown before dinner. For my troubles, I'd been promoted from serving maid to a chamber maid. When the queen next caught me helping the princess mend a torn hem with my bare hands, I'd been promoted once more to the royal seamstress. The pay was nonexistent, but the perks, namely coming to the capitol with a dress I made that would be on display, were life-changingly priceless.

"Do something with the nails and makeup. The prince likes red." With that, Queen Indira descended from the carriage in a flurry of silk and lilies. She barked orders at the guards to rest and water the pegasuses, leaving me and Charlotte alone on the front grounds of the castle.

I turned to Charlotte. Her normally mischievous features had paled. Her blue eyes were wide and unfocused as she stared past me. Her lips moved, but no sound came out. Finally, she whispered, more to herself than to me, "I can't do this."

"I can give you a quick manicure."

Charlotte reached for the door on the other side of the carriage. The queen was already disappearing into the castle's darkened doors. The ever-present Skykeeper guards that were always lurking around her had moved toward the servants' entrance. Relief in their sagging shoulders, as though glad to finally set down this charge now that the package was safely delivered to its new owner.

Charlotte was walking in the opposite direction toward the stone walls that surrounded the castle. The doors to the outside world were already closed. No one manned the massive battlements to reopen it.

"I can't do it, Belle. I won't."

For the first time since I'd known the fairy princess, I saw the cracks beneath her defiance—the desperation, the fear. I didn't know what to say. I stepped out of the carriage. But then turned back and grabbed for the wedding dress. The guards would return to stable this carriage while we went inside, and I refused to be parted from my ticket out of Evergrove. When I turned back around, Charlotte was yards away from me. I had to run to reach her.

"I can't marry that beast."

"I'm sure the rumors are an exaggeration. He's the son of a lioness. So he might have a big nose and sharp teeth. It's not like he's a troll."

Charlotte wasn't listening to me. She was eying the wall. The dainty fairy princess gathered the edges of her skirt. Her boots struck the wall with sharp, frantic sounds, recapturing more dirt than I'd just cleaned off. Her hands reached for the lattice as though it were salvation.

"Your Highness… Charlotte, stop!"

She did not stop. Her fingers clutched the tangled vines, and she began to climb. I took a step forward, but the gown slipped. I couldn't let it touch the ground. I couldn't let it wrinkle. I couldn't —

A flash of steel caught my eyes. The steel was strapped to Charlotte's upper thigh. The fairy princess' quite muscular upper thigh was exposed to the sunlight for all to see as she threw one strong leg over the wall, followed by the other.

I didn't know what bothered me most. The fact that the fairy princess had a dagger strapped to her thigh or the fact that there was no one around to help me as she hitched that exposed leg with the dagger over the wall.

"Charlotte, please!"

Charlotte looked down at me. Her arms were the only things holding her up. It was the first time I'd noticed the tone there on her biceps. I did manual labor every day of my life, and I didn't have that kind of muscle.

"I don't want this life, Belle." And then she was gone.

I stood there, frozen, my hands clutching the gown like a lifeline. The air felt too still, too heavy. My thoughts raced, but they all circled back to the same singular truth.

Charlotte was gone.

There would be no wedding.

And no one would see my dress.

CHAPTER TWO

ADOM

The pale stone walls of the Summer Castle were bathed in the warm glow of the setting suns. Solara's silvery light softened the sharper edges of the structure, while Lyra's rays warmed the air, casting long shadows across the sprawling lawns. It looked just as I remembered—serene, untouched, a world apart from the suffocating grandeur of the royal palace. A place of respite, of peace.

And now I was about to ruin it.

My breath fogged the glass of the window as I gazed out at the familiar grounds. My earliest memories were born here. My father's booming laughter echoing through the halls as he chased me through the corridors. The smell of sun-warmed grass and earth as I prowled the woods. I could almost hear the rustle of leaves beneath my paws, the distant calls of birds startled into flight as I practiced stalking through the underbrush, my father's shadow always close behind me.

I rubbed a clawed hand against my jaw. The coarse fur along my cheek rasped against my palm. Up in the sky, Avarix gleamed faintly in the sky, a crescent of cold light trailing the daughter sun. Ever in pursuit of Lyra, his eternal obsession, the First Moon chased her across the heavens. Soon he would be full. His face would glow bright and vengeful as the smaller sun once again slipped through his glaring beam. In his anger, he wouldn't turn inward. No, he would turn those icy moon beams down on the people of Solmane and demand a price for his failure.

It was a price I had saved years to pay. The debt was coming due now. It rolled toward the castle, gilded wheels on cobblestones, bearing the one thing Avarix had decreed would appease him.

My bride had arrived.

The receiving room was heavy with silence, broken only by the faint hum of Jorge's prosthetics as he shifted his weight. To anyone else, the sound was imperceptible, masked by the low crackle of the hearth and the distant chatter of a skeletal crew of servants preparing for the princess's arrival. But my ears, attuned to the smallest details, picked up the subtle whir of gears and the faint, rhythmic hiss of hydraulics. Jorge's enhancements were as much a part of him as his dark eyes and razor-sharp wit.

He stood beside me, one arm crossed over his chest, the other resting lazily at his side. The metal of his fingers gleamed faintly in the firelight. Jorge's human features were classically handsome: dark hair that was effortlessly tousled, a strong jawline, and a perpetual smirk that could charm or infuriate, depending on his mood. Beneath that smooth exterior lay a body built for war. Hidden blades, strength amplification, and tricks designed for seduction and killing alike. Or so the rumors went.

"Was this the best idea, Your Highness? There were reports of trolls in the woods a week ago."

"Much rather fight a troll than…"

"Than face your bride? No wonder this first date feels more like an ambush than anything."

"Don't be fooled. Royalty are the stealthiest and most cunning fighters in the world."

Jorge snorted at that, as though it were a joke.

It wasn't.

"I hear she's beautiful."

Jorge didn't need to say her name. I knew who I was marrying. Knew it since the day she was born almost twenty-one solars ago on a Hunter's Eclipse when Lunaterra passed between Avarix and Lyra. With the planet blocking the daughter sun's light, Avarix fell into shadow. Though the eclipse only affected Solmane, the First Moon's rage could be felt across the entire planet.

"It's a marriage of convenience. Her looks don't matter."

Jorge didn't respond. The unspoken truth hung heavy in the air between us. *My* looks mattered. What bride would willingly accept a husband who resembled a monster?

"There will be no courtship. No love." I spat that last word, but the bitterness lingered on my tongue. "I'm doing my duty—to the moon, to my people, and to end this war."

"Good for you, Highness. Love always ends in loss. If you're lucky, it's just the loss of an organ, like the heart. At worse, one lover must die first, leaving the other alone."

He wasn't wrong. Love had taken my father, hollowed my mother, and made me a beast with blood on my hands. This marriage wasn't about love; it was about fulfilling the demands of the curse so the moon might grant me what I craved most—the ability to fully shift. To shed this monstrous half-state and reclaim the humanity stolen from me at birth.

The curse wasn't the only weight pressing down on me. The trolls still prowled the borders. They were relentless and ravenous since the First Moon had withdrawn its protection from Solmane. Their raids had claimed my father and left scars on my people that ran deeper than flesh. If this marriage would return us to the right sight of Avarix's light, then I would see it through.

And yet, as much as I wanted the war to end, there was a part of me—the beastly part—that didn't want to lay down arms. The part that thrived in the chaos of battle. The part that longed for the feel of troll flesh beneath my claws and the rush of blood pounding in my ears.

"You're going to terrify the poor girl." Jorge's expression was thoughtful as he looked me directly in my eyes. Few men had the balls to do that.

"Precisely. I want her to see me, get her screams out of the way, and then move on to the wedded bliss portion of our lives together where we rarely see or speak to each other."

Jorge didn't argue. He didn't tell me to try and be pleasant to win her over. He didn't tell me everything would be all right. He simply blinked and twisted his lips in a thoughtful expression. He had a way of reading me that I found both irritating and useful.

The palace chamberlain entered the sitting room. Colson bowed his head. Then glanced up, meeting my gaze. "She's just freshening up, Your Highness."

A low growl of annoyance left my mouth. Neither Jorge nor Colson shuddered at the sound. They'd been with me too long. My bark was as bad as my bite, but they both knew I needed them to stay in my employ. Each man dealt with the parts of my duties that I preferred to ignore. If only one of them could take on my matrimonial duties.

I flexed my hands and then squeezed them back into fists, feeling the sharp tips of my claws bite into my palms. My reflection in the window was distorted. Surprisingly, it was an improvement. The gleam of my mane and the sharp line of my jaw were unmistakable. I looked like a predator preparing for the hunt.

Up in the heavens, the two suns were sinking below the horizon. All thirteen moons were visible even now in the twilight sky. They orbited Lunaterra, on the hunt for the sunlight they craved. Every night, the moons raced across the skies in pursuit of Lyra. Every night they failed to catch the daughter sun.

Because love was a losing game—even for the heavens.

CHAPTER THREE

BELLE

"No, no, no!"

I heard the queen's cries long before I saw her. The words grew sharper, louder, punctuated by the rapid clicking of heels against stone. The sound was a metronome of panic. The sharp clatter dulled to a muffled, uneven rhythm as she stepped into the unturned earth near the wall.

It was too late. Charlotte was already gone. The last swish of her white skirts disappeared over the lattice wall, leaving only the faint rustle of disturbed ivy and the soft thud of boots hitting the ground on the other side.

"Charlotte!" The queen's voice was a shouted whisper, the kind a parent directs at a misbehaving child while out in public. "You will come back this instant, Charlotte! Do you hear me?"

Queen Indira paused, listening, as though expecting a response. None came.

Her alabaster-pale face was flushed with fury as she turned to me. "This is your fault, Bess. I trusted you to keep her in line."

"Me?" The only line I kept with the princess was her measurements.

"Instead, you let this happen."

I wanted to protest, to tell her that I hadn't let anything happen, that her daughter was as uncontrollable as wildfire would be in the deserts of the Deadlands. Queen Indira didn't want excuses; she wanted someone to blame.

Her gaze dipped to the gown in my hands. I pulled it tighter to me. Queen Indira was a master at turning chaos to her advantage. I could see her mind working now, fitting the pieces of this disaster into something resembling a plan that would have her as the primary benefactor.

"It could work."

I didn't respond. Because I had no idea what I might be getting myself into.

"You share the same coloring," she said smoothly, her voice regaining its regal composure. "And from a distance, no one will know the difference."

I hadn't gotten the highest marks in school. I was far more interested in thread count and color combinations than math and literature. But I knew how to read a pattern, and I could see that the final product of the queen's designs would be a disaster that would unravel all around me.

"You'll pretend to be Charlotte."

Clearly, I would've gotten a gold star for my prediction. What I really needed was a healer to take the queen by her hand and tend her during her temporary insanity.

"You'll wear a veil. It's an old human custom. Something to do with protecting the bride from vengeful spirits—or other suitors—who might try to claim her before the vows were spoken."

The fairy queen tried to pull at the gown in my hands. That's when I found my voice.

"Queen Indira, I know you're upset. We'll find Princess Charlotte. Just send the guards after her."

"There's no time. The Beast Prince is waiting."

"I can't pretend to be a fairy princess."

"You can. And you will."

Queen Indira turned away and strode to the back of the carriage. Her hands deftly untied the straps that held the luggage in place. Where was that dexterity when the attendants had been loading all the trunks back in Evergrove? No wonder they'd all scattered to the servants' quarters the moment the carriage came to a halt. Within moments, Queen Indira had pulled out a lace veil, its delicate pattern shimmering faintly in Avarix's pale moonlight.

She draped the veil over my head. The material wasn't even good lace. Its uneven pattern betrayed a rushed hand, the inconsistencies glaring to someone like me who had spent countless hours perfecting the gown still clutched in my arms.

The veil wasn't delicate. It wasn't refined. It didn't match my carefully tailored dress in color or design. Where my gown was soft and luminous, this veil was coarse and dull, its edges poorly finished and curling in places where they should have been smooth. It was an insult to my craft, to everything I valued, and it was now on my head.

"He likely wants to sniff you. Or mark you. I hear beasts do that."

"Mark me? You mean bite me?"

"Just hold still while he has his way with you. You

obviously know what to do. It's not like you're pure like my Charlotte."

I wanted to snort, to laugh in her face, but I bit my tongue—literally, as the lace of the veil slipped into my mouth. Charlotte. Pure? The memory of one of our more candid conversations during a fitting flickered in my mind. Charlotte had known things that a proper fairy princess shouldn't know about her body and how it worked.

"Meanwhile, I'll send the guards to search for Charlotte. We'll have her back by dinner."

I opened my mouth to protest, to say something—anything—to stop this madness. The moment I did, the veil betrayed me again. The coarse lace slipped into my mouth. I gagged, the taste of dust and desperation sharp on my tongue.

"If you don't go in there, he could call it all off. Then no one will see your gown."

She had me there. I swallowed hard against the lump of lace in my throat. If I didn't go in there, if the prince called off the wedding, everything I had worked for—all the hours, the meticulous stitches, the aching fingers—would be for nothing. My masterpiece would vanish into obscurity, just as I feared I would.

"Give me the gown, Bess."

That was where I drew the line. "No one handles this dress but me. And it's Belle."

"No. It's Charlotte. At least for the next quarter hour or so. That's about as long as the act takes."

Wow, if that's all the action the late king gave her in the bedroom, no wonder she always looked like she had just sucked on a bitterbell bloom.

The queen gave me a push to the castle doors. I shifted the gown in my arms, adjusting it with practiced care. Inside, the Beast Prince awaited. People called him monstrous, cursed.

And he might bite me.

I wasn't sure what beasts ate. There were blood fae and mages who feasted on flesh. Stone shifters who I supposed ate rocks. Dragons who, if you believed the stories, preferred virgin sacrifices. I'd grown up with rumors that fairies were sweet, like the flowers we evolved from. There was truth to that in the carnal act. But outside the bedroom, I had no clue what we tasted like.

The beast came from a pride of lions. Those jungle cats were carnivores, right? Blood was savory, not sweet. There was only sap in my veins, not blood. Therefore, I couldn't be a delicacy. Right?

Chamberlain Colson gestured for me to step forward. His face held that practiced unreadable expression of the elevated servant class. I caught glimpses inside rooms as I trailed him down the hall. Outside, the castle looked abandoned, forgotten. Inside, it was like stepping into a museum. Every object was preserved but untouched. All around me were the echoes of a life lived in warmth and love, now muted by time.

My eyes roamed over the ornate furniture, the gilded frames, and the heavy drapery that seemed to drink in the dim light. Sadness crept into my chest. This house had known joy once, I was certain of it. Now it was as hollow as the footsteps I left behind on the marble floor.

Colson opened a door. I felt the queen step up behind me, but he held her back. The last thing I saw was the thunderous expression on her face before the door shut her out. Surprisingly, I didn't wish she was by my side as I stepped into the room. She was not the ally anyone would want at their back.

The faint light from a distant hearth flickered, casting long shadows across the walls. I could hear my own breathing in the quiet of the room. It was uneven and shallow, mingling with the creak of the floor beneath my feet and a strange whirring sound.

I gave my eyes a moment to adjust to the room. Movement stirred in the shadows. A figure emerged, tall and broad, his presence unfurling like a creeping vine overtaking its surroundings.

He wasn't what I had expected. Not with those chis-eled features and that piercing gaze. His broad shoulders and commanding frame were impossible to ignore, especially in his military uniform with all those medals and gold. He was handsome, but there was no warmth in his eyes. No softness. Only a cool, assessing look that made me feel like a butterfly pinned under glass.

"If you don't want to be queen, all you need to do is scream."

The air rippled around him, heavy with his presence. I forced myself to stand tall, lifting my chin in defiance. "Are you going to bite me now?"

The faintest flicker of confusion crossed his face. He looked at me like I was a clock showing the wrong time. "Remove the veil."

My fingers curled into the folds of the wedding gown. The familiar fabric grounded me. "Human custom dictates it's bad luck to see the bride before the wedding day."

His expression changed then. The cool mask dissolved into something… monstrous. This must be the beast everyone feared. He moved, sudden and fluid, lunging toward me as though to rip the veil away himself.

I staggered back. I reached for the door and wrapped my hand around the door knob. Before I could turn it, something shifted in the corner of the room. The flickering shadows twisted and came alive. A low, guttural sound rumbled through the air. My blood turned to ice.

The roar shattered the silence. It was so loud it actually shook the walls. It wasn't human. It couldn't be. It was a living, breathing beast with teeth sharp enough to tear me into many pieces.

CHAPTER FOUR

ADOM

Jorge and I had fought side by side for years. There wasn't a battlefield I could remember where he hadn't been at my back, his mechanical limb a blur of precision and strength. He'd risen quickly through the ranks, a feat for a mere human. His skill and cunning outpaced even the most vicious shifter. The man tore through trolls as though he had a personal vendetta against them. He was more than my second in command; he was my brother-in-arms, someone I trusted implicitly. Which is why I didn't stop him as he questioned my bride-to-be.

I'd seen him wrangle confessions out of hardened criminals. Sometimes with just his cheerful voice. Other times, he used his hand, which hid all manner of torture devices. The moment that hand reached out for the princess, something inside me snapped.

There was a tick in my left eyebrow. My incisors ground against one another. The claws at the end of my fingers felt like they were growing longer, slicing through more of my flesh.

The roar tore from my throat before I could stop it. I was on him before I processed moving. My claws left my palms and found Jorge's neck. I hauled him back, slamming him against the far wall. The impact cracked the wood paneling, sending a shudder through the room.

"Do not touch her."

The sharp edge of Jorge's blade hand bit into my arm. The sting was immediate. Hot blood welled against my furred skin.

I ignored it. Pain was nothing compared to the rage roaring through my veins.

"Something isn't right." Jorge's voice was tight with strain as I squeezed his neck. His dark eyes darted to the veiled figure with her back pressed against the door. "Show yourself."

I growled again. I didn't like Jorge talking to her. It pissed me off that he'd given her a command. He had the power to order my army around. But not her. She was mine.

It was that thought that had me loosening my hold on Jorge. *She was mine?* Where had that come from?

From the corner of my eye, I studied her—my bride. The scent of her reached me first, soft and sweet, like the gardens after the rain. The veil obscured her face but couldn't hide the lavender hue of her skin. Nor the gentle curves of her figure outlined beneath the fine fabric. Her dark hair fell in loose waves over her shoulders, a contrast to the pale lace that shrouded her features.

Shifters had no distinction between their human side and their animal side. We were one and the same. Unless they were like me and caught between the two. With the princess' scent in my nose, the human part of me lost its grip, and the beast stirred, restless and hungry. It wanted her—wanted to protect her, to claim her.

The princess had one hand clutching her chest and the other on the doorknob. "It's bad luck to see the bride before the wedding," she repeated.

Her fingers tightened around the knob. I expected her to turn it and dash out the door and into the night. She didn't. One by one, her fingers released their hold. She took a determined step into the room.

"I was trying to honor your father's human customs."

She held herself rigid, defensive. But she wasn't trembling. There was fear there, yes, but not panic. She wasn't afraid of me. She was trying to please me.

So she'd been prepared.

Both our families had known she would be mine since the day she was born. The Skykeepers had read the constellations and foretold that the Princess of Evergrove born on the Hunter's Eclipse would be bound to the Prince of Solmane. Our destinies had been written in the stars. Or rather, written by the moon. We could not escape each other.

Well, we could. We could defy the gods as my parents had done. But by her stance, I doubted Princess Charlotte would. Not when she was looking at the result of defying Avarix.

She wasn't looking directly at me, but her gaze landed close enough. I forgot the veil. Forgot Jorge's suspicions. Forgot the curse and saw only her. Her composure. Her strength.

She hadn't screamed at me. She had been frightened of Jorge's aggression, not my presence. A strange sense of relief washed over me, unexpected and unwelcome.

"Leave us."

Jorge hesitated, his jaw tightening. "Adom—"

"Now."

It seemed he might argue. Then he nodded stiffly. The faint hum of his prosthetics followed him as he stepped back. The mechanical parts of his body moved with a stiffness I'd never seen him display before. He cast one last look at her—sharp, searching—before exiting the room. The door closed with a soft click, leaving the two of us alone.

The veil shifted slightly as she moved, the lace catching the dim light. I caught a flicker of something beneath it—a glimmer of her eyes, watchful and assessing.

I couldn't see her features clearly, but I knew the weight of someone's stare. Hers didn't feel heavy. It didn't bear the usual burden of disgust or fear I'd come to expect. Instead, it felt… curious.

"I'm not going to remove the veil."

"I'm not going to bite you."

The faintest flicker of something crossed her stance —a hint of relief, perhaps. It couldn't have been humor. No one joked with me except Jorge. And most of the times it was him laughing at his own jokes.

Without thinking, I stepped forward. "Will you take my hand instead?"

The weight of her gaze shifted down to my hand. Her silence stretched long enough than was polite.

"Is there a problem?"

"Your nails. They could use a trim. May I?"

I just stared at her, caught off guard by the absurdity of the observation. I'd expected a flinch, perhaps even a shaky apology. "You want to trim my claws?"

"The tips are jagged. They might snare the fabric of my gown."

For the first time, I noticed she held a gown in her arms. It was the traditional yellow of a Lunaterran bridal gown in honor of the suns. The princess set the gown down on a chaise nearby. When she straightened, she took my hand in hers.

Her touch carried a faint hum of magic. It felt like the gentle flow of a brook. It was nothing like the wild, untamed power of the moons that coursed through me. I watched, fascinated despite myself, as the edges of my claws began to smooth and reshape. Her magic moved with precision. Each claw was polished to a perfect curve, the jagged edges disappearing beneath her touch.

When she reached the last one, she leaned back, inspecting her work. "There, that's much better."

I didn't look at my hands. I looked at hers. She had held my massive paws in her dainty lavender hands and tamed them. My claws were still claws—sharp, deadly —but now they were... Well, not pretty. They were clean and even. No one had ever touched me like that— deliberately, gently, without fear.

We were closer now. The firelight shifted enough so

that she could see my features clearly. No shadows. No hiding.

When she looked up, she gasped. I waited, my jaw tightening, my chest coiled with anticipation. This was the moment where her mask of composure would shatter. Where she would scream.

She didn't.

Instead, she gasped softly, her hand slipping from mine as she stepped closer. "That's it."

"That's what?"

"Your hair. That's the color my dress is missing."

Her words were so unexpected that they silenced the growl rising in my chest.

The princess reached up. Her fingers brushed against my mane. Her hands moved through the coarse strands as though she were studying the texture.

As she turned my hair this way and that, trying to catch the light, her scent traveled up my nose. I'd never liked spirits much. As someone who wasn't in full possession of their body, I didn't want anything taking away any more of my control. She was an intoxicating blend of wildflowers and honey warmed by the sun.

The scent of her curled in the air like smoke from a dying ember or condensation clinging to glass on a cool night. It wrapped around me, a snake slithering closer to strike. Her bite was the poisonous drug I feared. I found myself helpless to resist and eager to indulge.

"The dress is going to be perfect with it," she said softly, almost to herself. Her voice carried the kind of focus I'd only ever heard in warriors preparing for battle—or in craftsmen consumed by their work.

"You… need my hair?"

She nodded, still distracted, her fingers curling around a strand. "Just a few strands. It's the exact shade of Lyra's rays. The color is exactly what I've been missing. Do you mind?"

CHAPTER FIVE

BELLE

In under five minutes, I had already royally screwed this up.

I'd warned Queen Indira that it would happen. Now when she found Charlotte, if she found Charlotte—no, *when* she found Charlotte—the princess would have to pretend to know how to sew. Because that's what I was doing right now as her doppelgänger.

"You've trimmed my nails. You've taken my hair. But you won't let me see your face?"

"No, Your Majesty."

"Highness."

Oh, for shooting stars. That's right. He was a prince, not a king. Charlotte would know that. It was another mistake. My fingers twitched as I sewed strands of his hair into the cuffs of Charlotte's wedding gown. I had been right; the color of his mane was the missing touch, and now the dress would be spectacular.

"You won't let me see your face, but you have no problems with me seeing your wedding dress."

I twisted my lips. He couldn't see the action because it was hidden by the veil.

The prince sat beside me. Well, not exactly beside me. We sat on a courting bench. It was a curved settee, shaped like an S. So that a young couple could talk without any petal plucking going on. I sat at the top of the S, and the prince sat at the bottom. Or vice versa, depending on perspective.

The prince was massive. He took up every bit of the curve of the S with both his top and bottom. His thick thighs were man spread in a way that showed off his obvious prowess. His chest was so broad that he spilled over his part of the S into mine. If I didn't keep my arms pressed into my body, I would curve into his.

I had heard the stories, of course. Whispers about the Beast Prince, who walked like a man but was something altogether different. Part lion, part human, and altogether monstrous. The gossips got it wrong.

Prince Adom was a beast—undeniably, overwhelmingly so. Everything about him was big. His broad shoulders stretched against the threads of his dark blue coat as though it might split apart at any moment. The rich fabric clung to him, powerless against the sheer size of his biceps. His narrow waist tapered into an arrow that pointed directly at the core of him—commanding, unavoidable, impressive.

Likely too big for the likes of Charlotte.

Poor girl.

Poor, poor girl.

Unlike his sun-golden mane, his fur was tawny brown. There was a coarseness to his mane, but the fur on his face and hands was soft. I knew because I'd rubbed the hairs on his wrist by accident when I'd been trimming his claws.

I wondered if the fur was all over his body. Was it over his belly? I could see the outline of a six—no, eight-pack of abs. Was it over his legs and down to his calves that disappeared into boots so large they looked like they could crush mountains?

No, Prince Adom of Solmane wasn't beautiful—not in the way I had been taught to think of beauty. He was magnificent, majestic, magnetic.

"You don't find that ironic?"

The needled pricked my index finger, and I winced. "What's ironic, Your Majes—Highness?"

"That I can't see your face, but I can see the dress you'll wear to our wedding?"

"Well, I figure it's the two of them together at the same time that would be bad luck."

"On our wedding night, I'll see you without the veil or the dress."

I missed a stitch. I never missed a stitch. Sewing was as ingrained in my brain as walking. Though I doubt I could take a steady step at the moment if asked. My knees pressed together to stop the tremor running straight to my core. Weren't tremors supposed to go down, not up?

Prince Adom's nostrils flared like he could scent the nectar pooling between my thighs. His eyes were golden, like his mane, but darker, deeper, as if they held the elusive heart of the daughter sun within them. The low rumble vibrating in his chest sounded like distant thunder. Virility poured from him.

I gripped the folds of the gown tighter, grounding myself against the pull of him. He was overwhelming, imposing, dangerous.

For Charlotte.

"You truly aren't afraid of me?"

"Do you plan to hurt her—me?"

"And you don't find me revolting?"

"Revolting? No. Ill-tailored, yes."

Not for the first time tonight, I bit my tongue. I

wasn't used to talking to royalty. Even Charlotte hadn't talked much during our fittings. As a commoner, typically talking to other commoners, I was used to speaking my mind unfiltered.

Prince Adom leaned forward, his huge body entirely taking over my part of the S on the courting bench. "I've given you my hair and now you're trying to get me out of my clothes?"

It was a joke. I knew it was a joke. But the entrepreneur in me saw an opportunity. "Well, not these. But your wedding suit? Might I have it?"

"What for?"

"To tailor it."

"You tailor men's clothing?"

"Not me. My dressmaker. She's amazing. Her name is Belle. She's an up and coming designer in Evermore. She's come to Solmane with me, and she's going to be a star once everyone sees the dress she made me."

"I thought you made the dress."

"I… designed it. You know how we ladies have our hobbies. I'm good with stitching." I held up my handiwork as proof.

He ignored it, eyes on me as though trying to peer through the veil.

I forced myself to straighten, to meet his gaze with as much defiance as I could muster. I was playing

Princess Charlotte. The fairy was quiet defiance personified.

But I didn't want to defy him. I wanted him to speak to me in that growl of a voice of his. If he did, I'd do whatever he told me to do.

Of course I would. Because he was a prince, and I was a commoner. A commoner pretending to be royalty for the night. Tomorrow, I'd be back in my place, and Charlotte would be the one speaking with him, sitting with him, sleeping with him.

"You're bigger than I expected," he said.

Charlotte and I were the same size. That size was average for a fairy. When we were standing, I'd come up to Prince Adom's chin. But there was no mistaking that the Beast Prince filled the room with his presence.

"I could say the same about you."

His brow quirked, a flicker of amusement breaking through the intensity. It was fleeting, but it had been there. "Is that a complaint?"

"No," I said quickly, then bit my lip, giving my poor tongue a break.

The Beast Prince tracked the movement. "I'm not complaining either. I like that you speak your mind."

Another screw-up for Charlotte to deal with. Once they found her and brought her back. Charlotte was quiet most of the time. When she did speak, it often surprised me what came out of her mouth. Like the fact that the princess knew about oral sex.

Maybe that's why she'd run away. Some fae boy had kissed her between the stalks. Maybe he'd gotten so far as to poke her with his stamen.

"I know you were raised with the sole purpose to wed me."

She was? I didn't know that. Why should I? The royals didn't air their goings-on to common fae, like me.

"You were sent reports on what I liked to eat, to read. But it looks like you were able to carve some sense of your own self out of this ordeal."

Prince Adom looked at me expectantly. All I could do was nod my head. I had no idea that was Charlotte's childhood. I'd only come into the royal household a couple of years ago. If that had been her life, no wonder she rebelled. What woman wouldn't?

"I'm glad for that. One less life for this curse to have ruined."

Curse? What curse? I kept my mouth shut, finally mimicking the fairy princess I was pretending to be.

The spool of thread in my lap was empty. There was still a little ways to go in the cuff, but I was out of thread.

I looked up at Prince Adom. He shifted, leaning

forward toward me. The firelight caught the strands of his mane, turning them into molten gold.

The first time he'd offered his hair to me, I had gone at it with excitement. This time, my fingers trembled as I reached for the dainty scissors in my work pouch. The shears felt small and fragile in my hand, almost laughable compared to the sheer size of him.

I raised the scissors, hesitating just inches from his mane. His golden eyes remained fixed on me, calm and unblinking. He didn't flinch, didn't even glance at the potential weapon in my hand. There was no fear in his gaze, no caution.

My fingers brushed his cheek. I told myself it was an accident. A slip of the hand as I reached for his mane. Deep down, I knew better. It was deliberate. I wanted to know what his fur felt like if rubbed the wrong way.

It was soft no matter which way my fingers ran through it. My index finger tingled as it grazed his jawline. His fur was warm and silken, as though every strand had been spun from sunlight. My fingers itched to explore more, to trace the strong lines of his proud chin, to brush the dark circles under his eyelids.

I wondered what kept him up nights. Did he have anyone to hold him?

He didn't move as I snipped his hair. He just stared, his eyes boring into mine as though he could see through the layers of lace and fabric separating us. The firelight flickered, casting shadows across his sharp features, highlighting the quiet strength in his stillness. There was no growl, no threat—just an intensity that made my heart pound in my chest.

I forced myself to focus, to ignore the heat pooling in my cheeks and the urgent flutter in my stomach. My hand moved with practiced precision, the blades of the scissors slipping into his mane.

The strand fell into my palm, light as air. Without another word—because words would have broken this fragile thing between us—I turned back to the gown. My fingers moved on instinct, threading the golden strand through the fabric. It blended seamlessly with the intricate embroidery I had already completed.

The prince didn't say anything, didn't shift from where he sat. But I felt his gaze on me, steady and unrelenting, as I worked. My hands trembled again as I tied off the final stitch, my pulse loud in my ears.

"You're done?"

"I'm done."

"You've taken my nails, my hair. Do you require anything else of me?"

"Just your wedding suit. If you don't mind."

"So that we'll match?"

I nodded. "We'll give the people something nice to look at."

His smile fell. "Other than my face, you mean?"

I blinked up at him. The strong angles of his face darkened. I should've been frightened. I wasn't. I was flustered. "No—I—that's not what I said."

Prince Adom stood quickly. The loss of his weight on the courting bench sent me rocking. He reached out one massive paw to settle the settee. Then he bowed stiffly.

"I'll have the suit sent to you. I'll see you on our wedding day. Good night, my lady."

With that, he was out the room.

I had screwed up royally. Well, for Charlotte. Not for me.

For me, I'd just secured another job. Prince Adom was going to look amazing in the wedding suit once I got my hands on it. But there was a part of me that wished I'd get to have my hands on him out of the wedding suit as well.

CHAPTER SIX

ADOM

Her words followed me like an echo, burrowing into my mind and refusing to let go. *Give the people something nice to look at.*

She'd meant something other than my face. This cursed, beastly mug I'd been burdened with since my birth. The sight of me sent others recoiling in fear or disgust on a daily basis.

But... looking back... had Princess Charlotte recoiled?

I replayed the moment in my mind.

Yes, she had recoiled. Twice. Once when Jorge had

reached for her. The thought of my second with his artificial hand on her made my claws ache even in the dim light of my memory.

Charlotte had recoiled a second time. After I accused her of slighting my face. She'd been smiling before. I remember that so vividly because I was focused on those plump lips—lips I wanted to bite.

I'd promised her I wouldn't mark her. But it was all I could think about as she sat sewing my hair into her dress with that serene smile.

I wanted to bite her. I wanted her bottom lip to scar, right in the center. So all would see it and know that she was mine.

Then she'd winced. At my words. Not at my face.

The only explanation was that she'd been trained well. The daughter of a queen would know how to mask her true feelings. How to hide her fear or disgust behind a veneer of politeness. That was it. That had to be it.

And yet.

Her smile lingered in my mind, soft and unguarded. I shook my head, growling low in frustration. This woman was twisting me in knots, making me question myself. I never second-guessed myself. I couldn't afford to.

"Your Highness." Colson's voice broke through my

thoughts, steady and measured as always. "Shall I ready your steed for the journey back to Pridehaven?"

"No."

Colson raised an eyebrow but said nothing, waiting for further instruction.

"We'll stay the night. Send word to the palace. Have my wedding suit portaled to the Summer Castle immediately."

The Summer Castle's portal was out of use. Otherwise, I would've used it to travel between here and the palace. But there was enough energy for an inanimate object, like an article of clothing.

We'd stay the night so Charlotte could work on the suit. Once we reached the palace, everything would change. Duty would take over, and this strange, maddening woman would become little more than a pawn in the political game we all were forced to play.

Here, in the quiet of the Summer Castle, I could still question. I could still wonder. I could still look at her and try to decipher the truth behind her smile.

Did she truly think I was something nice to look at?

Queen Indira paced by the front doors, her silks shimmering with each anxious turn. The heavy fabric of her gown whispered against the polished floor, an impatient rhythm that matched the tight set of her shoulders. She was muttering under her breath, too softly for most to hear. My ears caught the clipped cadence of frustration—or perhaps fear.

When I stepped into view, she froze mid-stride. Her wide eyes snapped to mine, and for a single breathless moment, she looked as though she might bolt. Quickly, she recovered, straightening her spine and smoothing the silks of her gown with a forced grace.

"Your Highness, I trust you found my daughter meets your satisfaction?"

"The princess is well-trained. I am satisfied she will meet all my needs."

"You took the opportunity to… slack your needs with her."

Her tone wasn't a question. It was a confirmation. As though it was inevitable that the beast I was wouldn't wait for my wedding night to assert my marital rights.

We were two nights out from a sacred celestial event, so people would be rutting all over the land. Only those lovers who were bound, or who planned to be bound the night of the eclipse would share their bodies on the event of the Hunter's Eclipse. Like his twelve brothers, Avarix was a jealous god. He considered it blasphemous to worship another body while his was blocked from Lyra.

"I trust you kept the veil on during your tryst."

The game was already in play. It was all I could do to keep from swiping all of the pieces off the board and crunching them under my heel. "Madam, I am a prince of Solmane and a gentleman."

"Of course, of course." Her shoulders hunched slightly, her head dipping as though she were trying to make herself smaller. The satisfaction I felt was fleeting.

"We'll be staying the night. Ensure the necessary arrangements are made with your people."

Queen Indira's hands twisted the fabric of her gown before offering a stiff bow. "As you wish, Your Highness."

Cool air wrapped around me as I stepped outside. The two suns had long since disappeared below the horizon, surrendering the sky to the moons. Tonight, they reigned in full glory—thirteen celestial sentinels scattered across the heavens like fragments of an intricate mosaic.

Avarix hung low and heavy in the night sky. His pale surface gleamed brighter than the others, appearing unnaturally close. In two nights, Lunaterra would pass between Avarix and Lyra, casting the First Moon into shadow and bringing the long-anticipated Hunter's Eclipse. For now, Avarix burned with a jealous light, as though daring the planet to try and disrupt his eternal pursuit of the daughter sun.

Two nights. Just two nights until the eclipse, when the price would come due. My curse, my people, my fate—it all revolved around that single, jealous moon.

My thoughts revolved around another body of light. Charlotte. Or at least the image of her I had managed to piece together through the veil. I hadn't seen her face, not fully, but I knew, without question, that I could pick her smile out of a thousand strangers.

It had made me feel light. The feeling had been foreign. Transient, like starlight pooling in my palm.

I gripped the stone railing, claws scraping against the cool surface. The sound echoed faintly, swallowed quickly by the night. My hands were too large, too rough, too beastly for such fragile thoughts.

Her touch. That fleeting moment when her fingers had brushed my cheek, light as a whisper. It had been an accident, a careless slip as she reached for my hair. It had devastated me all the same. A blow more powerful than any troll's blade. I could still feel the ghost of it, warm and soft against my fur, a sensation that had burrowed deep and refused to let go.

My heart, my cursed, clawed, and weary heart was doing funny things. Things I didn't understand. Things I wasn't sure I wanted to understand.

She hadn't flinched at my face. She hadn't screamed at the sight of me. Or recoiled at my presence. She had touched me—not out of duty or pity but with curiosity, even care. She didn't hate me.

Love, of course, was impossible. No one could love this—this half-formed thing, this beast trapped between forms. But the idea that she might one day…like me?

I exhaled slowly, my breath misting in the night air. Maybe, just maybe, that day would come. Not now, not even soon, but one day. Perhaps it would be on our wedding night after the vows were spoken, after I kissed her lips and then claimed her body with mine. After those sacred rites, my curse would be broken. The next day I could come to her not as a beast, but as a man.

Maybe then she might allow herself to like me. Maybe then I might come to like myself.

The thought lingered until a bitter wind sliced through it. The acrid stench of rot and iron wafted in the breeze. It was faint, but unmistakable.

Trolls.

The horizon beyond the castle walls trembled with movement. A low rumble carried through the night—a sound too heavy, too deliberate to be the shifting of trees.

A small clatter at my feet pulled my focus. I looked down, spotting a loose stone that had tumbled from above. My gaze shot upward, and my breath caught.

Against the pale light of the First Moon, a dark figure clung to the side of the castle, scaling it with unnatural ease.

There was no time to think. Only to act. With a snarl rumbling low in my chest, I leapt into motion and launched into the night.

CHAPTER SEVEN

BELLE

"Still no word?" Queen Indira demanded of the fae guards in the doorway.

Both men visibly gulped as they towered over the diminutive woman. One, a tall man with a scar cutting across his cheek, bravely stepped forward.

"No, Your Grace. It's as if she disappeared into the ether. We worry… it may be foul play."

"You think someone has taken her?"

"There's a chance," the second guard, who had perfect skin and a square jaw, admitted. "The Summer

Castle is largely unguarded. There have been troll sightings in the area."

The queen's pale skin went ashen. "A troll? Here? This close to the capital?"

"We're not within the capital's walls, Your Grace," the tall guard reminded her. "The Summer Castle has little to no defense as the royal family no longer keeps residence here."

"You'd think the trolls would have some self-preservation to stay away with that beast here."

I pursed my lips together to preserve the words that would do no good to anyone. Prince Adom might look like a monster, but he was gentle, careful even. At least with me. Me—the woman lying to his face from behind a veil.

The sound of footsteps drawing near interrupted the tension. The queen spun toward me. "Put the veil back on," she hissed.

I grabbed the scratchy lace veil from the table and slipped it over my head just as Colson appeared in the entry. He carried a carefully folded garment draped over his arm. He bowed stiffly, his face unreadable as always, and placed the garment on the table beside me.

"The prince's wedding suit, as you requested, Your Highness." He bowed again and left as quickly as he had come.

The queen shooed the guards out behind the chamberlain. The door clicked shut, and I tugged the veil off again, but not before the coarse fabric caught on the strands of my hair. As soon as I was free of the lace, I reached for the suit.

It was white, pure and untouched, like the light of the moons on a cloudless night. There were no embellishments, no details, nothing to catch the eye. Just plain, stark white.

That wouldn't do. Not for a royal wedding. Not for the prince who would stand beside the most intricate garment I'd ever created.

"You are a little upstart, aren't you? While I admire you turning this to your advantage, you have more important things to concern yourself with."

"With respect, Your Grace, this is my concern. I'm a seamstress. Not a princess or a warrior. I'm not your daughter. I can't find your daughter. And I can't fight trolls. What I can do is make the prince look the part of a king next to the princess, who will soon be queen of Solmane."

Queen Indira's lips pressed into a thin line, but she didn't argue. Instead, she sighed and waved a dismissive hand. "Do what you must. Make him look… presentable. While you do that, I'll continue to worry about finding Charlotte."

The door closed behind her, leaving me alone with the bridal gown and the groom's suit. I ran my fingers over the fabric of the suit, assessing it carefully. The cloth was fine, but it lacked character, lacked life. It was a canvas, waiting for someone to make it extraordinary. If there was one thing I could do, it was turn scraps into splendor.

As a child, I grew up wearing threadbare garments so patched together they were barely fit to be called clothes. But my magic had a way of weaving wonders. I tailored those scraps until they shimmered with the illusion of finery. The fabric was still poor, its quality unchanged, but no one could tell by looking at it. And no one cared. My creations showcased my body's best assets, concealing flaws while drawing the eye to what was beautiful.

That was my gift: I could take the humblest material and make it sing, hiding imperfections and revealing hidden potential.

In Evergrove, after being hired by the queen to craft her and her daughter's gowns from nothing, I became known for this. I was sought after by everyone who had a wedding, a feast, or a festival to attend. But Evergrove was small, and its people were … let's call it humble. My work wasn't meant to languish in the confines of the small municipality of Evergrove.

Now with both the royal wedding gown and the prince's suit entrusted to me, my moment had come. When the royal court laid eyes on my creations, my name would echo through the kingdom. I would no longer just be Belle of Evergrove. I would be the most sought-after designer in all of Solmane.

I gathered my tools, my mind already racing with ideas. The prince would stand beside his bride, a vision of power and grace. He would not simply be seen. He would be remembered.

The room was quiet except for the soft snip of my scissors and the faint rustle of fabric as I worked. My fingers moved instinctively over his suit, tugging, folding, pinning, as though the fabric whispered its secrets to me. I didn't need to take his measurements with tape. My fingers remembered every line of his frame, every rise of muscle.

His broad shoulders had stretched the seams of his coat. I imagined him filling this suit out, the sharp lines accentuating the curve of pecs. He was more beast than man, yes, but his body... his body was a marvel.

I added gold thread to the pants, my needle gliding through the fabric with practiced ease. His thick thighs were the kind that could crush an opponent—or, perhaps, pin someone in place. If Charlotte didn't hurry back, I'd gladly take her place as his bride.

The needle pricked my index finger. I brought the digit to my mouth, horrified at myself. That kind of thinking was pure lunacy. Worse, it was treason.

I was nobody. A seamstress. A dressmaker. Not a bride. Not to a prince.

Figuring I must be lightheaded, I loosened the ties of my tunic. Immediately, I felt a rush of cool air as the fabric slackened around my shoulders and my wings came free. The purple petals unfurled from their cramped captivity. Iridescent veins shimmered within the delicate membrane, catching the light as they flexed, refracting hues of violet, indigo, and faint traces of gold. The edges curled slightly, soft as silk but edged with the strength of spun steel. As they extended fully, the ache in my shoulders ease and my brain cleared.

A faint sound at the window called to my attention. The sound was followed by a smell on the wind. The hair on the back of my neck stood on end as I turned, my needle poised like a weapon. Much good that would do against anything but a beetle.

The window creaked open. The night air rushed in, cold and sharp. A figure climbed through, moving with the calculated ease of a predator.

Jorge landed silently, his dark eyes locking on mine. His mechanical hand gleamed faintly in the moonlight. The hum of his enhancements filled the room with a low, ominous whir.

"I knew it wasn't you." His voice was low and dangerous. "Where is she?"

Before I could ask what he meant, a deafening roar

shattered the silence, shaking the walls. My heart leapt into my throat as Jorge spun toward the sound. His hand turned into a blade that unfolded from his arm.

The next moment, he was yanked back toward the window, a massive clawed hand gripping the back of his coat as another roar tore through the night.

CHAPTER EIGHT

ADOM

I didn't remember leaping onto the balcony, only the rush of air as I soared through the night. Two stories fell away. My claws closed around Jorge's throat before I even registered that we both were falling. Metal met my grip. The cold bite of his armor dug into my palms as I squeezed.

I hadn't caught him off guard. My second in command was too well-trained for that. I was the one caught off guard. By the sight of my bride…and her wings.

That's what went through my mind as we fell. The

princess' wings stretched wide behind her, luminous in the lamplight. Shades of violet and indigo rippled like twilight skies. They framed her, transforming her from the little fairy princess I'd rarely thought about to the vision of the vixen who would plague my every thought until my last breath.

I had known she was beautiful. Even veiled, her elegance had been undeniable. But this?

I'd only caught sight of her for a second. It had been a second too long. Entranced, I lost focus. Jorge shifted his weight in an attempt to throw me off balance. Gravity won against both of us.

We toppled backward off the balcony in a tangle of claws and metal. The ground rushed up to meet us. But even as we fell, I kept her in my gaze.

We hit the ground with a deafening thud, flesh and gears colliding in a clash of rage. Pain rattled through my ribs. I ignored it.

"Adom, it's not what you think."

I snarled, digging my claws deeper into his armor, seeking the soft flesh beneath. "I think you were trying to steal my bride."

"That's true." Jorge twisted a gear, and my claw hold snapped. "But not...*her*."

I didn't wait for him to explain the nonsense. I didn't care. Our bodies were flat on the ground, where I had the advantage.

My claw-tipped fingers curled against the earth. The pads of my feet registered the faint vibrations of his heartbeat through the ground. The weight of my body rested evenly, my posture low and deliberate, the way only a feline hunter could manage. My breaths came deep and steady, in the rhythm of an animal about to strike. I sprang toward him, going straight for his throat.

Jorge met me with a fist enhanced with steel. The metallic clang that met my chin echoed in the night. We sparred often in training, but this was different. There was no strategy, no restraint. I wanted blood.

"Adom, listen to me. She's not—"

My fist hit his jaw and shut him up before he dare said anything about my bride, my woman.

My claws raked across his chest plate, leaving deep gouges in the steel. Jorge countered with a blade that slid from his prosthetic wrist, its edge gleaming in the moonlight. I didn't doubt that Avarix was watching and enjoying the bloodshed.

Jorge's blade nicked my shoulder. I retaliated with a swipe that sent him sprawling, his body skidding across the dirt. One thing about Jorge; he was relentless. He hadn't survived the Convergence Games, been conscripted into the Solmane army, and risen through the ranks in just three short years to stand at my side for nothing.

The human rolled to his feet and came at me again, his blade whirring as it arced toward my side. "I'm not the villain in this story, Adom."

I caught his arm mid-swing, my claws clamping down on the metal. "It's General. You should expect a court-martial if you survive this night, soldier."

I aimed for his throat, needing his neck column to smile red to appease my rage. What if he'd touched her? What if he'd taken her?

A flash of movement stopped me from slicing into him. My bride stepped out into the night. And the world shifted beneath my feet.

Lunaterra was the seventh planet in the seventh galaxy in the Orion constellation. This particular constellation was known for its frequent celestial events. With Lunaterra having two suns and thirteen moons, the planet was a hub of astronomical activities. Besides the occasion of my cursed birth, none had ever moved me bodily like seeing the fairy princess standing in the moonlight.

She was unveiled. Her lavender skin glowed softly in the moonlight. Her violet hair cascaded like silk over her shoulders. Her green eyes were wide, her lips parted. Her beauty hit me like a blow to the chest. But it was her wings that robbed me of my senses.

They'd appeared deep purple in the dim light of the bedroom. Now they shimmered like living amethyst under Avarix's glow. The First Moon's light passed through them, illuminating veins of gold and streaks of indigo that wove together like a celestial tapestry. They looked like something plucked from a dream. My dirtiest, wettest dreams that woke me to a real, live orgasm.

Desire and longing knocked me back with the force of a hammer. I wanted to touch them, to feel their texture beneath my fingers. Were they soft, like the petals of the twilight blooms in the royal gardens? Or did they hold a firm strength, the way her presence grounded me while also making me want to fly?

I had two foes now. Jorge, who wanted to steal her from my sight, and Avarix, who cast his best light upon her.

"Go inside, or he won't listen to reason," Jorge shouted. At her.

I thought I'd reached my breaking point when he'd stepped into her window. The foundation of everything that I was, everything that I believed, shook when he raised his voice at her.

With a snarl, I swiped at his legs. My boot caught the weak point in his stance. He staggered, then took me down with him. As I scrambled to gain the upper hand, my attention to my task of gutting the only man I had ever dared called friend was diverted.

My nose twitched. The sharp tang of decay cut

through the blood and sweat of our attempts to rip one another's innards out. It was unmistakable. Trolls.

Jorge's brows furrowed. He'd scented them, too. We took our eyes off each other's jugular and looked toward the tree line.

Four trolls burst from the shadows. Their foul stench filled the air, a sickly blend of rot and swamp water. Jorge and I leapt apart, immediately taking defensive stances to confront the enemy head-on.

The trolls didn't move forward. They broke and circled around us. They were heading for her.

The princess.

I didn't think, didn't hesitate. I lunged for the first troll. My claws tore into its thick, leathery hide. Its scream was guttural. And short-lived. I snapped its neck with a satisfying crack of bone and tendon.

My momentum carried me into the second troll. My teeth sank deep into its chest. I ripped my head back with a roar. Blood sprayed, thick and acrid, across my fur.

Jorge engaged another troll. The long blade from his prosthetic cleaned nicely through the troll's arm, making the two dismembered bodies match. The creature howled. Jorge silenced it with another strike to its neck.

Three down. But there had been four.

The fourth troll was barreling toward Princess Charlotte. Its hulking form moved with terrifying speed. I roared, tasting the blood of its brother on my tongue. My muscles burned as I pushed harder, faster. The troll was nearly upon her. I wouldn't reach her in time.

Then Jorge was there.

He placed himself between the princess and the oncoming troll, his body a shield of flesh and steel. The troll's club came down, colliding with Jorge's back. The force sent him to his knees. With a swift turn, Jorge unleashed a blast from one of his mechanical enhancements. The energy sent the troll hurtling backward—straight into me.

It was a move Jorge and I had perfected on the battlefield. I caught the troll in mid-air. My claws closed around its throat. With one brutal motion, I ended its life. The creature's body crumpled to the ground in a heap.

Silence fell. My fur was matted with troll gore, the dark stains of its blood and the ichor of its innards. I turned, my eyes immediately searching for her.

Charlotte was clinging to Jorge, her face buried in his shoulder. I felt a stab of disappointment. Not that she'd sought protection in Jorge. He'd be dead soon. There was a part of me that wished she'd pulled a dagger and defended herself. Or that she at least hadn't turned away from the end of the battle. That had been some of my best work.

Princess Charlotte lifted her head. Her eyes met mine. It was then that I wanted her to turn away.

I wanted to turn away, to shield her from the sight of me—the beast covered in blood and filth.

She took a step forward. Then another. "Are you… are you hurt?"

Her fingers brushed my face, soft and tentative, wiping away a streak of troll blood. Her fingertip came away red. I wanted to kill the troll all over again for getting her dirty.

The warmth of her touch burned through the chaos, causing the planet to shift off its axis. My knees threatened to buckle. But I held firm, staring at her as though she were the daughter sun herself and I, unlike Avarix, had caught my prize.

I would never allow her to leave my orbit again.

CHAPTER NINE

BELLE

The carriage jolted as the pegasuses surged forward. At first, their gait was steady, measured—a canter that shook the wheels. Soon, the pace quickened. Muscles rippled beneath their gleaming white coats. Their nostrils flared as they leaned into the harnesses. The carriage swayed with each stride as their momentum built and their wings caught air.

In most places, pegasuses needed a longer runway to lift off with carriages. A clever young inventor from Evergrove had solved that problem with a lightweight, collapsible glider frame that could attach to the sides of the carriage. Made from tightly woven plant fibers and reinforced with thin but sturdy wooden ribs, the frame created additional lift by catching the air as the pegasuses flapped their wings.

They ran faster and faster still. The wind whipped through the open windows, catching my hair and tugging it loose. Their hooves left the ground even as they kept racing. We were lifting, no longer just striking the earth, but gliding over it.

I barely noticed the takeoff. My attention was fixed on the figure leading the charge. Adom.

We weren't flying high, just above the treetops. Adom's tawny hair gleamed in the moonlight, like he was the son of Solara. He was a blur of raw power, darting ahead of the carriage. Sometimes on all fours. Sometimes upright on his powerful legs. His mane of golden hair whipped wildly, a streak of brilliance against the twilight sky. His movements were fluid, feline. Each bound and stride exuded a controlled ferocity that was utterly mesmerizing.

Queen Indira sat rigid beside me, her sharp features marred by a scowl. She twisted the veil in her hands. The useless scrap of fabric wrinkled further with every angry tug. I couldn't bring myself to care. My world had narrowed to the sight outside the window.

Adom's head snapped to the side, his nostrils flaring

like he caught a scent. He slowed, scanning the land-scape with those piercing eyes before surging forward again. My chest tightened as I watched him. He was hunting. Protecting. Leading.

And it was all for me.

The power in his every move, the ferocity of his gaze as he searched for danger—it was all directed toward ensuring my safety.

He was magnificent. There was no denying it. A blend of man and beast in the most captivating way. Not beautiful, no. Beauty was too tame a word for someone like him. He was visceral, a force of nature that commanded attention and respect.

Heat rose in my cheeks. The beat of my pulse was visible at the underside of my wrist. It thundered in my ears, faster than the pegasuses' gallop. I tried to remind myself of the circumstances, of the farce we were playing out, but the logic was fleeting.

Watching Adom, his mane catching the light of the moons, his body coiled and ready to strike—it was impossible not to feel something. No, not something. I felt everything.

"This isn't a problem," Queen Indira declared, her tone making it clear she was convincing herself as much as me. "Once we find Charlotte, we'll simply swap you two back. He's a shifter. He won't notice. Animals think all fairies look alike."

Indignation bubbled to the surface. Prince Adom had been nothing but attentive and sharp in the brief time I had known him. Beast or not, he was no fool. His intelligence gleamed behind those piercing eyes. His loyalty was evident in every protective stride he took. He'd even threatened to maim his friend for daring to sneak into my window—something I should probably be thinking a bit more on, along with the fact that Jorge knew I wasn't Charlotte. But, really, why when I'd much rather look at Adom's backside as he tore across the countryside?

To hear the queen reduce him to something so base and unthinking made my stomach twist. I clutched the gown and his wedding suit tighter. It was my gown now.

I'd designed it. I'd labored over it. Charlotte hadn't cared one stitch for it.

The fabric pressed against my arms like armor. Adom deserved better than a queen who would manipulate him and a princess who would abandon him. He deserved—

"They've found traces of Charlotte," said the queen. "They should have her by morning. Until then, stay away from the prince. Do you understand?"

I didn't respond.

The pegasuses touched down in a gallop, their hooves striking the earth with a rhythmic thrum that gradually softened as the carriage slowed to a smooth roll. Pridehaven came alive outside the carriage window. It was a far cry from the woods and gardens of Evergrove.

The capital city bustled with life as shifters padded alongside fairies. Humans mingled with other beings I could barely name. A dragon trotted past with an ogre perched atop its back.

Glass spires reached toward the heavens, catching the eternal twilight of the equatorial suns and reflecting it in every imaginable hue. Each tower gleamed in harmony with the pale wood frames that supported them. Vines and blooming flowers clung to the buildings, their vibrant purples, yellows, and greens cascading over balconies like waterfalls. It felt as though the city had grown out of the ground itself, nature and civilization entwined.

Banners in deep crimson and gold draped across doorways and balconies, adorned with the crest of the Hunter's Eclipse. Vendors lined the avenues, calling out their wares: moonstone trinkets, eclipse pastries shaped like crescents, and ribbons of every shade meant to mark allegiance during the Convergence Games—an event that united the kingdoms in competition and glory.

The streets were crowded with people, carriages, and contraptions made of gears and steel. As our carriage rolled through the cobbled streets, they all parted. Conversations stalled, and footsteps paused mid-stride. The crowd parted like a wound opening. They stepped aside quickly, their gazes downcast as the Beast Prince prowled past.

Adom hadn't bothered to clean off the troll gore streaking his arms and tunic. His mane, wild and tangled with streaks of crimson, framed his face, casting sharp shadows under his golden eyes. He looked more beast than man, an apex predator surveying a world too fragile to hold him.

His growl rumbled low as he surveyed the crowd. His gaze swept over the streets like he was still searching for enemies, threats in his kingdom. There was something about the tension in his shoulders, the set of his jaw. I couldn't tell if it was defiance or guilt.

The journey through the main street was swift. With no obstructions blocking our way, we made it to Pridehaven Palace in no time. The structure rose like a living monument at the heart of the city. Walls of polished sandstone shone golden in the moonlight. The castle's spires were capped with domes of iridescent crystal, as though Avarix had gifted pieces of himself to crown the Lioness Queen's domain.

The carriage rolled to a stop, the heavy creak of the wheels settling as silence blanketed the air. My fingers twitched against the fabric in my arms, anticipation and anxiety warring within me.

The door swung open to reveal Prince Adom. Without a word, he reached for my hand. I gave it to him. His grip was firm but careful, as though he feared I might break under his strength. His claws grazed my palm as he guided me out of the carriage.

He turned to Colson, who had stepped forward to assist Queen Indira. "Show the queen to her quarters."

"Thank you for your security and hospitality, Your Highness. The princess and I will retire immediately for a night's rest." Queen Indira's hand fluttered in a come-hither motion at me.

Prince Adom didn't let go of my hand. "The princess is coming with me. She'll sleep in the queen's quarters."

Queen Indira faltered. Her practiced composure cracked. Her lips parted in protest, but no words came. She twisted the useless veil in her hands until the garment tore.

CHAPTER TEN

ADOM

I knew I was squeezing her hand too tightly. She didn't protest. She didn't tell me to stop. Nor did she pull away.

She followed me. Willingly. Her smaller hand rested trustingly in mine.

Each step she took alongside me loosened the grip of tension that had wound itself around my chest. Servants stopped their cleaning and dusting and general movement and bowed their heads as we made our way down the hall and up the staircase to the private quarters. The deeper we got into the palace, the more I calmed.

She was safe here. No one and nothing would take her from me.

My heart rate slowed to only three beats a second once we reached the king and queen's chambers. I paused at the queen's bedroom door, glancing down at Charlotte. Her gaze flicked to the heavy wooden panels, then back to me. There was no fear in her eyes.

I pushed the door open, stepped inside, and pulled her in with me.

The room had been my mother's. Now it was a tomb of memories. It hadn't been used since my father's death, two decades past. I rarely slept in the palace. When I did, I kept to the barracks with the other warriors. The queen's room had been cleaned and prepared for our wedding night. After we said our vows and sealed the promises with a kiss, we would come here and consummate the union.

The thought had me turning to Charlotte. The sudden movement caught her off guard. She flinched, her purple wings fluttering like a startled bird preparing for flight.

The small reaction gutted me. I dropped her hand and took a step back. "I disgust you."

"No. It's the blood. I told you—I'm no fighter. I like pretty things. Clean things."

The gore of the trolls still clung to my fur and tunic. The run to the capitol had taken some of it, but streaks of dark red and patches of viscera remained. The pride I usually felt in my strength, my savagery, was gone.

"I'm neither of those things; not pretty or clean."

"No," she agreed. "You're strong, fierce, and deadly."

Her words surprised me with their honesty. She wasn't smiling. She wasn't trying to placate me. She simply spoke the truth.

We had nothing in common. I was strong, fierce, and deadly where she was pretty, dainty, and clean. How was this ever going to work?

The palace advisors, the Skykeeper Mages, my own mother and the fairy queen had been feeding Charlotte details about me her entire life. What I liked to read. What I liked to eat. The political views I held. They were all determined to make her the perfect shadow that would attach to my heels and live as a castoff. Reflecting me and having no opinions or thoughts of her own. Guilt had dogged my conscious for years at this notion. Until the moment she opened her mouth and asked for a strand of my hair.

This fairy had a mind of her own and a will to match it. Watching her sew a part of me into her dress had sealed both our fates. No matter our differences, there was no way in the two suns that I would let her go.

"You're fierce, too."

She blinked at me. Her wings fluttered as she pressed a hand to her chest. "Me?"

"You ran toward the trolls. You didn't scream. You didn't hide. You didn't think of yourself. You're not a fighter, but you still fought."

I'd been disappointed that she hadn't pulled a dagger to defend herself. But on the run here, I realized she could've done far worse. She could've run into the danger and been hurt. Instead, she ran to my side but stayed back while I fought.

Her eyes roamed over my face, taking their time as they surveyed my mane. "You're wrong. You are pretty; your mane is very pretty."

She reached up. I felt more than saw the tingle of her power as she magick'd the gore out of my hair. She wiggled her fingers, pulling away the grime, the dried blood, and troll gore that had clung to me like a second skin. Her magic didn't sting or burn. It was gentle, light as a breath.

"Your shoulders are so broad and sculpted—I want to tailor a coat for you."

Her palm rested on the sleeve of my arm as though taking my measure. The filth and stains vanished from my tunic like they'd never existed. The threads shimmered, the weave tightened and mended beneath her touch.

"I feel your strength, but you're so gentle with me."

Her words unraveled me, one thread at a time. I stared at her, torn between awe and a desperate kind of ache. No one had touched me like this before—with care, with reverence. Her words, along with her touch, scraped against the walls I'd built, breaking through piece by piece.

"I like your growl."

I hadn't realized I'd made a sound.

"It curls my toes. And—"

I didn't let her finish. I pulled her to me. Her head got buried in my chest. My fingers were inches away from her wings. I couldn't help myself. I let one finger brush against the bottom of one wing.

She inhaled sharply.

The sound sent a jolt of panic through me. I started to pull away, convinced I had scared her, hurt her. But I couldn't move. Her hands were tangled in my mane, gripping tightly, refusing to let go.

I could have easily broken her hold. But I didn't. Actually, I couldn't.

She wasn't scared.

She wasn't disgusted.

She wanted me.

Her wings fluttered again, this time opening wide as though she were showing them off. Her palm settled flat against my chest, right over my heart. The warmth of her touch burned there, far deeper than fur or bare flesh. She sank into my core.

My hand curled roughly around her wrist to stop her. "Don't."

"Are you hurt there?"

Once again, I didn't answer. I couldn't. She should know; this wasn't a love match. It couldn't be.

She looked into my eyes, like she saw straight through me—past the walls I had spent years building, past the armor I thought impenetrable. I had stood unshaken on countless battlefields, faced beasts and trolls without flinching. But here, before this fairy with no training in war, I was defenseless. She wielded no blade, only her gaze, and I felt myself falling—terrified of the power she held over me, terrified that I wanted her to wield it.

"I want to be your bride, Adom."

She said my name uncertainly, like she wasn't sure she had the rights to it.

"I don't have a lot to offer—other than my loyalty and my tailoring magic. I can promise you that you'll be the best-dressed prince in all of Lunaterra."

Her laugh was self-deprecating. Her tooth caught her lower lip, and she chewed at it, looking at me uncertainly. Didn't she know this union was a done deal? Neither of us could back out of it. Not without dire consequences. The consequences would be damnation if she dared to even try to get away from me.

"I have your scent. If you run, I will catch you."

Something wild sparked in those green eyes of hers. Challenge? Anticipation? Maybe both. It wasn't fear. All this time and she had never once smelled of fear of me.

"When you catch me?" She tilted her head back, her hair brushing against her cheek. "What then?"

"I will devour you like the beast that I am."

She gasped. This time I knew it was delight. I knew it because that spark in her eyes ignited, and she grinned. At me. Had any woman ever grinned at me?

The moment between us stretched, taut and electric. Until she broke free of my hold and ran. Her laugh was the chime of a bell as she darted away. Her wings fluttered at her back, but not enough to give her flight.

She didn't get far. Barely a few steps before I was on her. My arms closed around her waist as I lifted her off the ground.

Her laughter cut off mid-giggle. I turned and threw her onto the bed. The new linens crinkled beneath her weight. She propped herself up on her elbows, her wings once again open wide and on display for me.

I loomed over her, my shadow stretching across the bed as I placed my hands on either side of her, caging her in. "You didn't get very far."

Her lips parted, her cheeks flushed as she met my gaze. "I didn't want to."

My claws brushed against the delicate fabric of her gown. Of course, they snagged in it. She didn't flinch, didn't shy away. Instead, her hand lifted, her fingers trailing through the mane at the side of my face. The touch was light, reverent. It burned through me with a force that left me raw.

I couldn't hold back any longer. My lips crashed into hers. She'd said something about gentleness earlier. Whatever imaginary beast she'd conjured that performed that action was not in this room. Her lips were sweeter than anything I'd ever tasted, sweeter than unrefined sap. Fairies had evolved from flowers under Solara's gentle rays. This fairy princess was the goddess's most perfect creation.

And she would never know that this was my first kiss.

CHAPTER ELEVEN

BELLE

Adom kissed me like he'd never tasted anything sweet before. He kissed me like I was the rarest nectar and he was parched beyond reason. The intensity of it was all-consuming, leaving no room for thought or doubt. My world narrowed to the heat of his mouth on mine, the possessive press of his tongue, and the way his sharp teeth grazed my bottom lip, sending sparks skittering down my spine.

I'd never been kissed like this in all my years. Fairies were known for their unique taste. It was said that we tasted like honey to shifters and humans.

I'd never kissed a shifter. Kissing a human was considered taboo in Evergrove. To most fae, humans were a step below shifters and barely a step above trolls.

Didn't matter. I didn't want to ever kiss any other being again after being kissed by the Beast Prince. When he finally pulled back, I was breathless. My pulse fluttered like the wings at my back. I thought that was it; that we were about to get naked and get to the main event.

I was wrong. Adom was just getting started.

He brushed the lightest touch of his claws against the base of my wings. My entire body shivered in response. He stilled immediately, his golden eyes darting to mine.

My wings were made of strong stuff. They could handle the wind's harshest torrents, the sting of rain, and the scrape of brambles. And yet… I couldn't find the voice to tell him so. I was too caught up in the way he looked at me—as though I was the most precious, beautiful thing he had ever seen.

His claws traced along the gossamer edges, the gesture so painstakingly gentle I shivered again. Adom's gaze followed every shift and flutter. I didn't need to give my consent vocally, not when my body was being so loud with its desires.

Adom leaned closer. His head dipped, his breath a

warm whisper against the membrane of my wings. The moment his lips touched them, I thought I would shatter apart. A single kiss, feather-light, more reverent than anything I'd heard spoken in a temple. The sensation rippled through me like lightning across water, leaving every nerve alight.

I was going to faint. I was sure of it.

He kissed my wings again. More aptly, he licked them. The same way he'd kissed me, like I was his first taste. His lips tasted the delicate veins with the same care one might give a rich dessert. My skin burned in response. My hands flew to his shoulders, fingers curling into the fabric of his tunic as I tried to anchor myself.

"Adom…"

His hand cradled the back of my head. His lips captured mine again. This kiss was hungrier than the last. When his teeth tugged at my bottom lip, I knew I'd let him bite me. Mark me. I wanted it to scar. So that every being on this planet knew that he was mine.

My fingers tangled in his thick mane. I couldn't seem to stop touching his hair. The golden strands were impossibly soft. I curled my fingers tighter, trying to pull him down to my neck. Was that where shifters marked their mates?

Adom growled low in his throat. His mouth left mine for a heartbeat, his breath warm against my cheek as he drew in a deep, ragged inhale, like he couldn't get enough of my scent. Then he was back, his lips slanting over mine with renewed fervor. But I wanted them at my neck, staking his claim.

"Adom," I breathed against his lips, the word a mix of plea and surrender.

He pulled back just enough to meet my gaze, his eyes burning molten gold.

"Aren't you going to mark me?"

"Before our wedding day?"

"Does the day matter? I'm yours."

He purred at that. An honest to goddess deep rumble from that massive chest. I wanted him to make that sound when he licked at my core.

The bite could wait. I needed him inside me right now. I reached for his trousers. His large hands surrounded mine, but they didn't stop me.

"I want to. I want you. I want you all for myself."

"It'll hurt." He looked down at the clear outline of the beast in his pants. The sight of the impression made my mouth water even more than his purr did. "I'll hurt you."

"I'm not a virgin."

Adom blinked. Then blinked again. His eyelids lifted slower this time, as though my words did not compute.

"Oh." Now it was my turn to wince, and partially shutter my eyelids. "Are you?"

"Of course not." He sounded scandalized. His brows knitted together as though he couldn't fathom how such a question had even crossed my mind.

Fairies weren't known for abstinence. Was he expecting his bride to be pure? If so, that was hypocritical.

"I have experience. You do, too. We both know what we're doing. Which means this sexual encounter is not going to hurt me. Unless you wanted a virginal pure princess. Because I'm not that."

There. I'd told him. Well, it was a partial truth about not being a *particular* princess.

It was a start. I'd get to the other bit soon enough, especially since I doubted the guards and queen would find Charlotte. The actual princess clearly didn't want to be in this position that I very much wanted to be in.

"Who?" he demanded.

"What who?"

"Who touched you?"

"Are we swapping names of former lovers now?"

Adom gritted his teeth and growled at me. I merely blinked and waited patiently for his temper tantrum to pass. It wasn't like Charlotte was innocent. No matter what, he would've gotten an experienced woman.

"The point is, I'll be the only woman you ever sleep with from this day forward. And you'll be the only man who ever touches me until my last day in the sun."

That appeared to appease him. His big shoulders relaxed. His lips were still pursed, but he was no longer grinding his canines. And the growl had—well, the growl was still there. But I had plans for his mouth that included growling.

I reached for his pants again. But he grabbed my hands, careful of his claws. I stared at the hand over mine, marveling at how well my lavender skin went with his tawny gold fur. I couldn't wait to see us naked together. I would design a whole line of lavender and golden brown couture.

"What is it now?"

"The fact that we both have experience doesn't change the fact that I'm huge."

"Yeah? Show me."

CHAPTER TWELVE

ADOM

My cock was twitching in my pants. It strained at the fastenings, eager to part the curtains and put on a show for her. I wanted her. Desperately.

Her kisses were a heady drug. I was far past drunk on them. I had expected fear, hesitation, even disgust. But all I saw in her wide, glimmering eyes was desire—pure, unflinching desire. She kissed me like she enjoyed it, like she wanted me.

I had bedded actresses. Women who pretended they wanted me, when what they truly wanted was a favor or coin. I used them as they used me, granting them a favor, or handing over payment and then slacking my lust with their bodies.

Charlotte had asked nothing of me. Except to see my cock.

Her lips were swollen from our kisses. Her chest rose and fell as she gazed at me from the bed. Her hair spilled over her shoulders like liquid silk. Her wings were spread out on the pillow. She looked like an offering, a gift from the gods who I had only ever known to be cruel.

"I'll turn out the lights." I reached for the nearest wall sconce. My claws brushed the gas valve, ready to extinguish the light.

"Why?"

Her question stopped me cold. Surely she didn't want to see me, all of me. I was a monster, and monsters belonged in the dark.

"Why would you turn out the lights?" She tilted her head, her expression curious, soft. "If you do, we can't see each other."

I wanted to see her. I never wanted her to leave my sight. That wasn't the problem.

"So you don't…" My tongue felt thick in my mouth. "So you don't have to see me."

Her brows furrowed as though I'd just spoken nonsense. "But I want to see you."

My claws curled into my palms as I fought to process her words. I shook my head, my mane brushing my shoulders as I looked away. "I don't want you to be afraid."

She moved then. Her scent enveloped me along with her arms—warm, sweet nectar. Her hand rose to cup my cheek. I closed my eyes and leaned into her palm. She had no idea how she had laid me bare. She could've gutted me in this moment, and I would've thanked her for holding my guts in her hands.

"I'm not afraid of the dark, Adom."

"You're not afraid of me, either. Are you?"

"Why would I be afraid of you? You won't hurt me. I watched you tear apart four trolls that threatened me. Then you growled at and terrorized any and everything that moved on the road tonight because it got too close to me. Fear of you is the last thing I'd ever feel. I know I'm safe with you."

I met her eyes, searching for the lie. There was none.

That was when I knew. Knew, with absolute certainty, that I was in trouble. I wasn't supposed to feel the thing blooming inside my chest. But as her hand lingered on my face, as her words settled deep in my chest, I was helpless to it.

My heart left my body and latched itself on to her. Forever.

I sprang off the bed and tore off my clothing. She

gasped, but I knew it wasn't at my body. It was at my actions. She looked at the fabric as though offended by my treatment of the garment. Then she shrugged, likely because she knew she could fix it and tailor it better. I looked forward to having her dress me, but first I wanted to undress her.

"Yeah, you are a big boy, aren't you?" Her gaze had left my discarded clothing and rested on the restless beast between my thighs.

I grinned as I lifted her dress off, careful to not tear any of her buttons or fabrics. She lifted her arms over her head, completely trusting of my every motion. She'd read me right; fear was the last thing she ever need feel for me. I would give my life to keep her safe.

She spread her thighs, letting my big body settle between her legs. It felt like home.

My cock pressed against her core. The tip of that massive beast wept with gratitude. She was wet, but not enough for the likes of me.

In the past, women had lathered themselves with ointment to receive me. I had none here.

I stared down at my claws. The sharp, curved talons had defined me since birth. I'd come into this world with them out, scratching my mother's womb as I emerged—a cursed child from the very start. These claws had been my greatest weapon, the tools that had kept my people safe and my enemies at bay. But now, looking at Charlotte's soft flesh, they felt like a curse all over again.

My choices were to work my massive cock into her inch by painstaking inch—and I had a lot of inches on me. Or draw blood as her intimate muscles clenched around the sharp points of my claws.

"Please, Adom, please."

The sound of her begging would've brought me to my knees if I wasn't already on them. Her legs were spread obscenely wide on either side of my thighs. I watched her beautiful body writhe beneath mine. Purple and tawny brown, how beautiful together.

She reached down to her sex and parted her folds. Oh, how she glistened for me. Still, it wasn't enough.

"Put your fingers inside yourself."

She did as she was told, placing her index finger and middle finger into her core. They pumped in dry and came out sopping wet. Sweet fucking nectar. The slurping sound of the suction had me swallowing hard. I couldn't wait to get my mouth on her, but my cock demanded its due.

"That's a good girl. Add a third finger."

She did as she was told. Her low back arched up off the bed, pressing her ass into the mattress as she did so. Her wings fanned out, beating in time to her fingers pumping in and out of her. She was close, and I couldn't wait any longer.

I snagged her wrist and pulled her hand away from her core. I placed her fingers in my mouth at the same time as I pressed the tip of my cock into her. We both lost our breath.

"Good?"

My sweet princess mewled like a kitten. No, not a kitten. She was too courageous to be a kitten. She was a lioness cub. With wings. A sphinx.

I growled low in my belly as her nectar slid past my tongue. I sucked her fingers as I pressed myself forward, stealing another inch into her. Her nipples were the deepest purple, near black. I ran one of my canines over her index finger the way I wanted to handle the peak of her breast.

"Okay, okay. You're big. No, no—don't withdraw. Just let me catch my breath."

"Don't stop breathing, little sphinx."

"I can't fit both you and my full lungs in my body at the same time."

I chuckled. She did too. Leaning down, I captured her laugh with my lips. She tasted like pure sunshine.

"We're gonna do this." Her eyes were dark pools of desire as she looked at me.

"Have sex? It certainly looks that way."

"I mean, we're going to get married."

I gathered both her wrists in one hand and pulled her arms over her head, trapping her. "I told you, if you run, I will catch you. Your scent isn't just in my nose. It's in my mouth. It's down my throat. It's on my cock. You're inside me, little sphinx."

Her body undulated beneath mine. She wasn't trying to get away. She was trying to take more of me into her. "I'm going to like being yours. I'm going to like it very much."

Every word that came out of her mouth was not what I expected. She was not what I expected. She was everything I never dared hope for.

The next time she shifted her body up, I pressed deeper into her. She breathed through the invasion. We breathed together. Until I was settled deep inside of her.

When I was, I just held there, staring at her. She stared back. Neither of us said anything. We couldn't fit words between us. So when she was ready, she nodded.

I withdrew to the tip. We both inhaled into the vacuum left behind. I had every intention of taking it slowly, to be gentle. Halfway through the first thrust, I lost control over that plan.

My body rushed back into hers, hating any parsec between us. Her cry emptied her lungs of any remaining breath. I filled her to the brim, then pressed impossibly deeper, craving more of her. We both took a shallow breath as I only barely withdrew from her a second time. She clenched around my length, trying to hold me inside her. That's how the battle began.

My thrusts became rapid fire. Each retreat was shorter and shorter as I advanced deeper and deeper into her. She held the line, clenching her inner muscles so hard that I whimpered in defeat as much as I groaned in triumph. When her first peak hit her, the detonation set us both back on our heels.

A roar loud enough to be heard by all thirteen moons tore through me. I released my heart, my soul, my very being into my bride. For the first time in my life, I sent up a prayer of thanks to Avarix for forcing my hand and giving this gift to me.

The moon was right. She was the perfect choice for me. In the morning, the curse would be broken, and I would come to her as a full man.

CHAPTER THIRTEEN

BELLE

The faint sound of grinding woke me. It was a sharp rasping that scratched at the edges of my dreams. I blinked in the dim light of the room, trying to adjust to Avarix's shadows. The sound continued, steady and rhythmic, like stones scraping together.

Adom lay beside me, his broad form barely contained by the bed. His mane spilled over the pillow, catching the moonlight that filtered through the window. But it was his claws that held my attention.

He was grinding them together. It was the sharp tips rasping against one another. I reached out, resting my hand gently over his claws. The grinding stopped immediately.

"Did you have a nightmare?"

His expression was dark, as though he was caught in some private torment. "I've lived a nightmare my whole life."

I tightened my hold on his hand, twining my fingers around his claws. I brought his hand to my lips, pressing a kiss to the back of his knuckles. "I'm here now. I'll chase the nightmares away."

I expected him to laugh, or at least grin, at the notion of a tiny fae protecting this hulk of a man. He just stared at me, his eyes unguarded in a way that made my chest tighten. There was so much in his gaze —pain, hope, fear—that I couldn't look away.

"Adom?"

Finally, he spoke, his voice rough and low. "I'm sorry."

"For what?"

"Things will change once we're wedded. Once we properly exchange our vows under the moon."

"I am completely, incandescently happy with how things are right now."

His claws twitched beneath my fingers. His lips almost formed a smile, but it didn't reach his golden eyes. He pulled me closer, his arm wrapping securely around my waist. I loved the feeling of safety he surrounded me with. Though he held me tightly, I couldn't deny I was falling.

Falling into him. Falling in love with him. Falling asleep inside the safety, protection and care he gifted to me.

When I woke in the morning light, the space beside me was empty. Adom's scent lingered on the sheets—wild and earthy—but there was no sign of him. I sat up, wondering if I'd dreamed the entire thing, if the Adom I'd seen in the middle of the night, so raw and unguarded, had been a figment of my imagination.

My thumb brushed the back of one of my knuckles. The warmth of his touch, the echo of his claws against my skin, was still there. It had been real.

The morning began with a whirlwind. I had no idea how they knew I was up, but as soon as I swung my legs out of the bed, a small army of servants invaded my room. They moved with practiced efficiency, their chatter a soft hum punctuated by the occasional clink of metal tools. Most of them were human—I could tell because they didn't carry the musky undercurrent of fur or the floral scent of fae beneath their skin. A few bore the technological enhancements that many humans adorned themselves with.

One woman's eyes were reflective glass. As she worked on my makeup, I saw my face in the mirrored surfaces. Her steady hands brushed color onto my cheeks and lips.

When she finished, I barely recognized myself. My lavender skin shone luminous. My hair was a cascade of carefully arranged waves, glinting like spun silk in the morning light. I felt like a doll, polished and painted.

Colson arrived to escort me out of the queen's chamber. He handed me a folded piece of parchment. "Your itinerary for the day, Your Highness."

The title still sounded foreign to me, as though it belonged to someone else. Because it did. Charlotte didn't want to be a princess, much less a queen. I knew exactly what I wanted, and that was the prince. If I had to wear a crown and have people bow to me to get him, I suspected I could endure it.

I unfolded the parchment and scanned the neatly written script. My eyes snagged on one line: *United Houses Luncheon.*

The United Houses Luncheon was a spectacle I'd only ever read about in the glossy pages of my favorite fashion zine. Every three years, the matriarchs of the allied houses descended upon Pridehaven with their unmarried offspring in tow, determined to flaunt their wealth, forge alliances, and secure advantageous matches. It was a marriage mart, plain and simple, cloaked in the pretense of diplomacy and tradition.

The event coincided with the Convergence Games, where dignitaries and rulers came to the capital to watch the competitions, engage in meetings, and strengthen their alliances. But the luncheon? That was where the real battles were fought—not on the field, but in silken gowns, jeweled tiaras, and finely tailored coats.

For weeks afterward, the fashion pages would be filled with commentary, critiquing every choice of fabric, every cut, every bead and feather. The most daring ensembles were immortalized in sketches, while the less inspired choices were mercilessly mocked. As a child, I'd eagerly poured over those pages, dreaming of the day my designs might grace the spreads.

"It's customary for the Lioness Queen to attend, but her majesty is otherwise engaged. She requests you attend in her stead."

I opened my mouth. And closed it. I couldn't say what I wanted to say, which was that I'd never attended a fancy luncheon in all my life. My lunches were always taken in servants' quarters, where gossip and bawdy jokes rang around the room. I had no idea what do say or do in a room full of royals other than "Would you like your glass refilled?"

Colson gave a curt nod of approval before stepping back to let me continue on my way. But not before calling out six words that rooted my designer heels to the floor: "Your mother will join you shortly."

As if summoned by his words, Queen Indira appeared, gliding toward me with a smile so tight it could have snapped. She looked immaculate, as always, but her eyes betrayed her—hard and cold, calculating beneath the veneer of civility.

"Any word?" I asked softly, my voice carrying just enough weight to show I cared, but not so much to expose my anxiety over Charlotte's return.

"No."

That was all the fairy queen said. She showed no emotion, leaving me to wonder if she cared if her daughter had run and was hiding, never to be found. Or if something more sinister had happened to her.

The idea of Charlotte lost to the ether, or worse, was a bitter pill to swallow. She didn't deserve either fate. The poor girl just wanted to live her life on her terms. Personally, I was pretty happy with the terms of her life.

"I've decided you will continue this ruse until I achieve what I came for," the fairy queen was saying.

"And what is that, exactly?"

"None of your concern. Once you're married and I have what I want, then I do not care what becomes of you. You can stay with the beast or run like Charlotte."

"I'm not going to run."

"Of course you're not. You've had a taste of power."

I didn't bother explaining that I didn't care about the power. I just wanted the prince. I knew she wouldn't understand, let alone believe me.

The grand dining hall was a masterpiece of stone and light. The ceiling stretched impossibly high, its arched beams etched with intricate carvings of the moons and stars, as if the heavens themselves had been invited to dine. Long tables were laden with golden trays of delicacies I couldn't name, their mingling aromas—spiced meats, honeyed fruits, and roasted roots—creating an intoxicating scent. But it wasn't the grandeur that stole my breath.

It was the silence.

The moment I entered, all conversation ceased. Dozens of eyes turned toward me—sharp, assessing, predatory. I felt their weight like a physical force, pressing down on my shoulders, my chest. I struggled to maintain the composure I'd watched Queen Indira drill into her daughter.

Shifter eyes flashed first, their irises glinting like molten gold or silver in the light. Predatory and piercing, they scanned me with an intensity that made my skin prickle. Their nostrils flared subtly, as if they were scenting the air, gauging my worth. I fought the urge to step back, to flee under the power of their animalistic scrutiny.

The fairies were no kinder. There were a few ember fae, though none had their wings out as Queen Indira had once accused. Shadow fae sat poised and still, their gazes narrowed, lips pressed into thin lines. Their disdain was palpable, a cold undercurrent that seeped into my bones. The sea fae were bejeweled and beautiful. Beside them, I felt dull, insufficient. An impostor.

Then there was the dragon. I hadn't noticed her at first. Her human guise was flawless—until it wasn't. She turned her head toward me, and the faintest shimmer of scales rippled over her neck. The glittering bronze wave caught the light and held it. When she exhaled, smoke curled from her nostrils.

With each step I took into the room, I waded out of my depth. Another foot forward and I'd be drowning. The doors closed behind me and, like sharks scenting blood, they pounced.

CHAPTER FOURTEEN

ADOM

"The celestial alignment approaches. Avarix draws near, and the eclipse must not pass without fulfillment. The curse demands resolution. We urge you to keep your word."

There was only one person standing in front of me. But the Skykeeper Mages always spoke in the third person.

They urged me to keep my word? Did they think I wouldn't marry the woman the moon had blessed me with? Did they not hear my roar of pleasure last night? Did they not know the vows had already been whispered in the dark, sealed in sweat and the sweet sound of her sighs?

Probably not by the looks of them. This Skykeeper Mage had a crescent-shaped hood over their head. They spent their nights chanting to the moons in what had looked like a carnal fervor to me, the one and only time I'd gone into their temple. That had been the night that the moon revealed the name of my bride-to-be.

"I will keep my word."

"And the princess?"

My canine snagged on my lower lip as I thought about my fairy with that mane of violet hair and those lush lavender wings. She was a sphinx—my sphinx. The sight of her in our bed, rumpled and sated, was the only way I'd ever leave her side. That parting would always be temporary.

"Princess Charlotte is willing."

She was more than willing; she was eager. Not more eager than I was. Right now, she was late, and my impatience was starting to show.

"We thank you for your sacrifice, Your Highness."

Sacrifice. That word clung to me like a second skin. I'd been both its noun and verb since the moment of my conception. My parents' love had been a defiance of the celestial order, and I was the price paid for their rebellion. The moon had marked me as a sacrifice, my body warped by its curse. I had sacrificed my childhood to the whispers of pity and fear, my humanity to claws and teeth. For years, I had used this beastly form to keep the people of Solmane safe, their last defense against the endless tide of trolls.

No more. The curse would be broken. The moon's favor would return. I had finally found what I needed to be whole. And there she was, walking toward me.

Her lavender skin glowed as Lyra's rays peeked in from the windows. She wore a gown of deep emerald green, its color a perfect contrast to her skin tone. The fabric hugged her figure before flaring at her hips. Delicate gold embroidery trailed along the hem like vines. Her hair was pinned up, but loose curls framed her face, teasing the nape of her neck. I wanted to reach out and take it all down, just to watch the curls cascade around her shoulders, to lose my fingers in their softness.

She was biting at her lip, too. Unlike mine, hers was a nervous nibble. Her gaze was downcast. She was fidgeting—Charlotte, who had stood boldly before me with scissors and defiance, now looked unsure of herself.

I closed the distance between us in three strides. "What's wrong, little sphinx?"

Her eyes flicked up to mine, wide and full of uncertainty. "I… I failed you."

I didn't bother with more words. I pulled her closer,

wrapping her inside my embrace where nothing would hurt her. My claws didn't even snag in her fabric this time.

"The luncheon. I was a disaster. I mixed up the forks. I spoke to the wrong person in the wrong order. Most of the time, I didn't know what to say. I sat there like an idiot while everyone talked over me. I don't know politics. I don't know how to… how to be what you need."

A laugh rumbled in my chest before I could stop it. I felt her wings ruffle beneath their bindings. I wanted to free them, wanted her to never hide any part of herself from me. Instead of freeing her wings, I captured her mouth.

She stiffened in surprise but melted into me within seconds. Her hands found their way to my chest, and her small claws snagged into the lapels. Her lips were soft, sweet, addictive. I wanted to lose myself in her for hours, and I would. As soon as we faced our toughest challenge of this day, and that wasn't a snooty luncheon.

"My *little sphinx*. I don't care if you mix up the forks or speak to the wrong person. I don't care what kind of impression you make. The only thing that matters is that I like you. The rest of them can hitch a ride on a comet's tail."

"Okay." She nodded but scrunched that perfect

button nose like she didn't like the taste of the word. "That's the court. But… what if your mother doesn't like me?"

"My mother probably won't like you. She doesn't even like me."

Charlotte jerked back. She didn't get far. I had her hand in mine.

I pushed on the towering doors of the throne room, not giving her a chance to back away. I felt the faintest tremor in her grip. I brought her hand to my mouth and kissed her fingers as she'd kissed my claws in the middle of the night when I'd woken to find the curse still possessing me.

The fingers of her free hand pressed against my heart. The faint hum of her magic stirred the air between us. The coarse weave of my shirt softened. The material smoothed over my shoulders, tightening just enough to hint at the breadth of my chest without constricting. The hem adjusted itself, falling cleanly at my waist, and the collar molded to frame my neck with an elegance it hadn't possessed a moment ago.

"Perfect," she said, more to herself than to me.

I stared down at the shirt, then back at her. She had sculpted the garment directly onto me, each stitch perfectly aligned, every seam flawless. She had fixed my clothing, then looked into my beastly face and called me perfect.

I wanted to take it back. I wanted to take her back to the luncheon and find every shifter, fairy, or human who had been mean to her and fillet their skin from their bones.

"We do not linger in doorways. We enter with purpose or leave without hesitation. Indecision has no place in a throne room."

Queen Amara wasn't sitting on her throne. She sat on a chaise near the window, her back straight, regal, every inch the Lioness Queen. Her skin was the color of fertile earth after a spring rain, smooth and rich. Her hair spilled in wild waves of gold, brown, and black—a riot of untamed power that used to glow with life but had dulled over the years of her grief.

She didn't look at me. Her gaze, as always, was fixed on the painting that hung next to the empty thrones over the seat where my father had sat next to her for ten years.

Her fingertips danced over the vial at her neck. I'd opened it once when she was sleeping. My nose still wrinkled at the scent of poison that went up my nostrils and down my throat.

"Mother?"

Her gaze snapped up, and I caught it—the flinch. It was slight, a flicker in her golden eyes, but it was there. It always was. I barely reacted nowadays.

"Is this her then?"

Charlotte stepped forward, her lavender skin catching the light in a way that made her look like a figure carved from amethyst. She curtsied, graceful despite the tension in her movements. "Your Majesty."

My mother's gaze sliced over her like a blade, assessing every inch with cool, unhurried precision. "At least she's something pretty for you to look at." Her tone was devoid of warmth or approval. "She'll break this curse, and then this tiresome ordeal will finally be over."

It had been fine—bearable—when my mother was dismissive of me. I'd learned to endure it. But seeing her treat Charlotte with the same careless indifference stung.

"What curse?" Charlotte asked.

I'd assumed Queen Indira had explained everything to her daughter. Just as I'd assumed Charlotte had been schooled on my preferences in all things. Clearly, I'd been wrong. I reached for my bride, taking her hand gently in mine as I searched for the words to explain.

"Oh, Adom, you've done it now. The one thing I warned you not to do."

For the first time in years, my mother was looking me in the face. She rose from her chaise, her movements slow but deliberate. Her golden eyes, so much like my own, narrowed as she approached. When she reached me, her hand came up to my cheek. The touch was almost tender, but her words carried no such kindness.

"The point was to obey, not to fall in love. The moon will punish you. "

I flashed my eyes at the queen, a low growl rumbling in my chest.

She ignored what I'm sure she considered a tantrum and turned her ire on my bride. I braced myself for my mother's vitriol, preparing to block Charlotte in any way necessary.

But the queen said nothing. Her lips pursed. Then she turned sharply, her silks swishing around her as she swept from the room without another word.

"Adom? The curse? Is something wrong? Is something going to happen to you? Are you going to be okay?"

I pulled this perfect gift into my arms. I understood why dragons would burn whole cities and commit genocide. I'd do the same if anyone threatened my treasure.

"My mother was supposed to marry a fairy from your land. It was part of a pact that Avarix decreed generations ago. But she fell in love with my father when they were just children. He was human, a man who had no claim to the moon's favor. They married, and when I was born, Avarix cursed me. He left me like this—caught between forms, neither man nor lion. But the curse didn't stop with me. The moon took its protection away from our lands. The trolls invaded, tearing through our borders unchecked."

Charlotte opened her mouth as though she wanted to ask a question. But then appeared to think better of it. She placed her hands on my chest, right over the heart that beat for her, and let me continue.

"The curse can only be broken when I marry the fairy princess that Avarix chose for me. You were born on the next Hunter's Eclipse after my father's death, marking you the woman that the moon chose for me. When we exchange our vows, Avarix will restore his favor and his protection. I'll be able to shift into man or lion at will, no longer caught between forms."

Charlotte's fingers clenched into my shirt, as though trying to hold on to me. Which was why her next words confused me. "What if I refused to marry you?"

"The trolls would continue to swarm, their entire brood eventually getting past the border of Solmane. The soil of Evergrove will remain fallow. Some mages think Avarix will think up even more creative punishments for our lands. And I would remain stuck in this beastly form for the rest of my days."

Charlotte pursed her lips together. Tears pricked the corner of one eye. I caught the first one before it could fall by pressing my lips to her eyelids. She let out a sob, and I pulled her closer.

"We don't have to worry about that. Because it's you. And it's me. We want each other."

I felt dampness against my cheek. Why were more tears spilling from her lovely eyes? I tucked her head against my chest so that she could feel my heart beating for her, so that she would know the depths of my feelings were all for her.

"My mother was right; I love you. Last night, I thought the curse might have broken when I made my vows to you, but I suppose Avarix will wait until he gives Lyra chase during the Hunter's Eclipse before he breaks his curse on me. Once he does, I'll come to you as a whole man. A man worthy of you."

Charlotte jerked out of my hold, staring up at me in horror. "Don't say that. Don't you dare say that again. You are more than worthy. You're my whole... everything."

She reached up and brushed her fingers against my cheek. She ran her hands down my chest. I didn't think I had any knots left, but the last holdout unraveled something deep inside me. This little sphinx had more power over me than the mightiest of moons.

"You're my whole everything too, Charlotte."

CHAPTER FIFTEEN

BELLE

I adjusted a stitch along the hem of the wedding gown, which was difficult because my hands were trembling. The dress, once a symbol of my ambition and dreams, now was a cruel mockery of everything I'd wanted. My fingers knotted into the delicate fabric as I thought of Adom's words.

The curse. The moon. The lives depending on vows I couldn't fulfill. My heart pounded, each beat a reminder of the weight crushing my chest.

I rose, pacing the room. My feet ached from the long day spent in uncomfortable shoes that I couldn't fill. Charlotte's feet were smaller than mine. Despite my magic giving me space in the shoes, my toes still came away cramped. The physical discomfort was nothing compared to the storm raging inside me.

My mind replayed every moment since I'd met him. Adom, with his broad shoulders and those golden eyes that saw me—not the veil, not the deception, but me. He'd been so hopeful, so certain, and all I could think was *I'm not her. I'm not the fairy princess he needs to break this curse. I'm not his salvation.*

I'm nothing.

But he'd looked at me like I was everything. And I wanted that. I wanted to be that to him for the rest of my life.

I stopped pacing and looked at the dress again. The gold thread shimmered like the moon he was cursed by, mocking me with its beauty. I couldn't do this. I couldn't stand at his side, knowing I would doom him further. That I might even make it worse for the fairies back in Evergrove.

The Lioness Queen was right; love was a punishment, a curse.

I yanked the dress from the table, tossing it onto the floor in a heap. A few of the delicate beads came undone and scattered across the wood. The sound felt like something inside me had broken, too. I wrapped my arms around myself, trying to hold it together, but it was no use. Tears slid down my cheeks, hot and unrelenting.

No one would see the gown now. I didn't care anymore.

A sound came from the window. It was a soft scraping, almost like claws against glass. My tears halted as fear jolted through me.

What was it at my window now? Trolls? Jorge? I couldn't decide which possibility sent a colder chill down my spine.

Adom was away, tending to his duties. We wouldn't see each other until the eclipse. There was the old human superstition that he wasn't supposed to see the bride before the wedding. Bad luck, they said. As if luck had ever been on our side.

My gaze caught the sharp edges of the scissors on the nightstand. I snatched them up, clutching them tightly as I moved toward the window. I held the scissors out like a dagger, ready to defend myself.

The window creaked open. I tensed, raising the scissors higher. A figure climbed through, and I prepared to fight.

"Belle, it's me."

"Charlotte?"

The fairy princess tumbled through the window in a clatter of limbs and fabric, her entrance the furthest thing from regal. Her tattered cloak caught on the frame. She kicked herself free, landing with an unceremonious thud on the floor. Then she sat there, her chest heaving as she caught her breath.

"Charlotte?"

She began brushing herself off as though surprised dirt could possibly cling to royalty. Even covered in dust and wearing flat shoes—flat shoes!—she somehow managed to exude the aura of a princess. I didn't even know fairies could wear shoes without heels, not with our notoriously high insteps. Yet here she was, flat-footed in a torn cloak and streaked with grime.

"I need your help."

"You…" I pointed at her. "…need my…" I pointed at myself. "…help?"

I stared at her, my mind catching up with her sudden reappearance. And then, all the emotions I'd been bottling up since she fled over the wall erupted.

"You need my help! You ran away. You left me to marry the prince."

"I never told you to marry the prince. That was your decision."

"Your decision left me with no choice. Your mother shoved a veil over my head and told me to go to him because you were gone. What was I supposed to do, say no to your mother?"

"I find it better to just say nothing at all and then run away." Charlotte climbed to her feet but not before seeing the wedding dress on the floor. She picked it up, eying it appreciatively. "The dress did come out nice."

"Nice?" I echoed, my voice a low growl. "Nice!"

"We don't have time for this." Charlotte set the gown down and stepped forward with the regal impatience of someone used to being obeyed. "I need your help. It's about Jorge."

"Jorge? The human who tried to kidnap me?"

"He thought he was kidnapping me, not you. But it doesn't matter now. He's in trouble, and you're the only one who can get him out."

I gaped at her, disbelief coursing through me. "You think I'm going to help you? After everything you've done?"

"Yes," she said simply, her chin lifting in defiance. "You have to."

I laughed bitterly, crossing my arms over my chest. "I don't have to do anything. You can't order me around anymore, Charlotte. I'm not your servant."

"You're not a princess, either."

"No, I'm nearly a queen."

We stood there, staring each other down. The tension crackled. Neither of us was willing to back down.

Charlotte's gaze was the first to soften. Her hands fell to her sides. "Please, Belle. If you don't help me, Jorge will die."

There was desperation in her eyes. Over the past couple of days, all eyes had been on me. Queen Indira's glare, cold and calculating as she had demanded my help without a care for the cost to me. The Lioness Queen's gaze, void and detached, weighing whether I would break the curse that held her son in its grip. Adom's eyes, tender and hopeful, that I might possibly want his clawed hands and his boundless love.

All I cared about was Adom's wants. The cruel truth was that I couldn't give him what he needed. Not what he wanted most in the world.

"I'll help you." I forced the words out, each syllable like a knife in my chest. "On one condition."

CHAPTER SIXTEEN

ADOM

The room was cloaked in darkness, but to me, it might as well have been bathed in sunlight. One thing about being born with the eyes of a big cat was my ability to see in the dark. My gaze swept dispassionately over the familiar outlines of my chambers: the tall wardrobe near the window, the low table with a book spread open on its surface. I ignored it all as I glared at the closed door to the queen's chambers.

I'd never opened that door before. It had been empty all the years since the king's quarters had been mine. I swore I could feel her on the other side.

The wood was sturdy. I could break it down with one swift kick of my boot. It probably wasn't locked. Not that that detail mattered. I wasn't supposed to go in there, wasn't supposed to see her until our vows were exchanged during the eclipse.

There were ancient customs and rituals at play. The Moon had already cursed my life; I wasn't about to invite more misfortune by breaking tradition. And yet, the door called to me like a siren's song, urging me to cross the threshold, to see her, to hold her—

I exhaled sharply and turned away, heading to my bed. Not hers. Before I'd taken the first step, I froze.

There was a lump in my bed. A fairy-sized lump with the hint of purple wings peeking out of the covers. She was here. In my bed. Like I'd conjured her up.

Her head rested on the pillow that had cradled my restless dreams for years. Her hair spilled across the sheets in dark waves, catching the faint glow of the moonlight filtering through the curtains. Her breathing was steady, her chest rising and falling in a peaceful rhythm. The tips of her wings fluttered every few seconds.

She shouldn't be here. And yet, the sight of her felt like it was meant to be.

My claws flexed at my sides. I stepped closer, carefully, as though I might shatter the illusion if I moved too quickly. The scent of her grew stronger, filling my lungs with every breath. She smelled of flowers and earth and mine.

"Charlotte? Little sphinx?"

She stirred at the pet name I'd given her. Her eyelids rose slowly. For a moment, she seemed disoriented, her green eyes searching the dark. Then they landed on me.

"Adom."

My name had never sounded like a smile. Like the answer to a prayer. It had always come at the end of a scream of terror as courage or breath left a foe's body.

"You shouldn't be in my room before our wedding day. You're breaking the rules."

"I don't care about the rules. I needed to see you, to be with you."

My claws brushed against that lower lip that could command anything of me. She didn't flinch, didn't pull away. She leaned into my touch and kissed the tips of my claw.

"We have a few hours before night turns to day. I promise I'll be gone before then. I won't do anything to jeopardize the breaking of the curse."

Her words unraveled me, thread by thread, until I was nothing but the beast she had cured with nothing but a friendly smile. My hand trembled as it cupped her cheek, claws grazing the soft curve of her jaw. I had spent years commanding armies, holding the line against trolls, mastering every impulse to ensure my people's survival. But here, with her, I was undone.

I leaned in, close enough to feel the warmth of her breath against my skin, the faint floral sweetness that clung to her like the bloom of spring. I told myself to be careful, to be patient, to savor this moment like a starving man offered a single bite. My hunger was too great. I could only think of how long I had been starved of such tenderness. Since the day my father died, no one had looked at me with anything but duty or fear.

"I wanted to see you in your wedding suit."

The absurdity of it struck me, and I laughed. A deep, rumbling sound that shook loose the tension coiled tightly in my chest.

Charlotte climbed over me and reached for the suit I hadn't seen on the chaise. This woman had truly gotten past my defenses. She'd snuck into my room with armor. Under her command, I stripped myself bare, offering her every bit of vulnerability.

She watched me, biting her lip as I stepped into the wedding suit. The fabric felt alien, nothing like the coarse tunics or battle leathers I was accustomed to. It was soft—too soft—like woven moonlight against my skin. The cut was exact, tailored so precisely to my frame. The snug fit over my thighs made me hesitate, unused to clothing that hugged rather than armored.

Charlotte's hands brushed over the waistcoat,

adjusting it with careful precision. Perhaps copping a bit of a feel. Not that I minded. I stood still under her gaze, more exposed than I had ever been in battle.

"Well?" The fabric stretched slightly over my shoulders as I spread my arms. "Do I meet your expectations?"

"You look…magnificent."

There was that lip bite again. It was going to make me throw the suit off.

"Now take it off."

Clearly, my bride and I were on the same page. I smirked and did as I was told. I figured she'd want me to place the suit back in its garment bag. But she was on me before I had the shirt over my head. She unbuttoned the trousers and pushed them down my thighs, her knees bending to follow the fabric down.

She took my cock in her hand, and I hissed. She didn't give me any more warning than that. She took me from hand to mouth, swallowing as much of me as she could manage.

I roared.

So much for traditions and rituals. Charlotte hefted my heavy sack with one hand and the base of my cock with the other. With two hands and her tongue, she brought me to the brink and then stopped. She pulled off me with a pop of her mouth. Then the slip of a fairy pushed me onto the bed. I fell with a mighty crash.

She stripped the nightgown from her gorgeous body with the hand that had nearly unmanned me. The sight of her naked had my cock weeping in surrender as her wings fanned out behind her. This was how to bring the Beast Prince to his knees.

I wasn't even on my knees. She had me flat on my back, begging for mercy.

My little sphinx showed me none. She mounted me, spreading her lavender thighs over mine. I arched up, spreading her obscenely wider.

I didn't need to ask if she was ready for me. My big nose scented her arousal. My cat eyes saw her pink folds glistening. She slid down onto me with ease.

Well, mostly with ease.

It took a moment and some movement, but my fairy took all of me inside of her. Once she was fully seated with me completely inside her, we took a single breath together. And then we began to move.

I thrust up, which caused her wings to flutter. She ground down, which caused my claws to dig into her hips. Faster and faster we rode each other until I swore we were flying.

"I love you, Adom. You have all of my heart, always."

I couldn't form words. The beast had my tongue. I could only growl as I thrust up into her tight sheath. This fairy would be the death of me, and I'd go happily.

She clenched her intimate muscles in time to my thrusts. The spasms became erratic, the grip on my length tighter. She arrived at her peak and was about to go over. I gripped her tighter to me, my claws drawing blood as my little sphinx threw back her head and roared her pleasure.

"I am yours body and soul. From the moment I met you and until the day my soul no longer gives light, I am yours, Charlotte. I love you."

A sob burst from her chest, mingling with her cries of ecstasy. Silent tears followed the sob. They slid down her cheeks like rain on glass.

I understood the feeling. I had not expected our union to be like this. Reversing our positions, I pulled her beneath me and kissed each of her tears away. My cock was still hard inside her. Her thighs were locked around my back, her arms locked around my neck. There was nothing for me to do but rock gently into her until she reached a second and then third peak. Once she was spent, I finally loosened the hold on my own pleasure.

There was no roar this time. There was no need. There was no competition to warn off. No enemies daring to near my territory. The mating ritual was complete, save for the spectacle we'd engage in the next morning with the whole of Solmane watching.

Right now, she was simply mine. And I was hers.

The moon hadn't lifted its curse. It might not ever. It didn't matter.

There was a lightness in my chest, a sense of being tethered to something more meaningful than curses and moons. What I had now, what Charlotte had given me, was more potent than anything the moon could grant—or take away. I wasn't whole in body, but I was whole in spirit.

CHAPTER SEVENTEEN

BELLE

The servant's dress was scratchy and too big. The coarse fabric clung to all the wrong places. My wings were pinned inside. They ached from the confinement, but I couldn't afford even a flicker of magic to alleviate the discomfort. I needed to blend in, to be invisible.

The streets of Pridehaven were alive with unrestrained joy. The entire city was caught in the thrall of celebration and anticipation. Overhead, the Hunter's Eclipse loomed massive and luminous, its pale crescent edge slowly turning black as Lunaterra began to pass between Avarix and Lyra.

Banners of gold and white hung from every window, the sigils of Adom's royal house rippling in the soft breeze. Flowers were everywhere—lavender and white lilies, their heady scents mingling with the aromas of roasted meats, sugared pastries, and spiced wine. Children darted through the crowd, their laughter rising above the strains of music played by a troupe of fae musicians on a nearby stage.

Dancers spun in circles, their movements as bright as the sunlight glinting off their sequined costumes. A shifter in wolf form howled at the darkening moon, and the crowd erupted in cheers. The rhythm of the drums thrummed in my chest as I weaved through the revelers, keeping my bonnet pulled low over my face. The air buzzed with energy and the promise of something greater—a union that would bring peace and prosperity, or so everyone believed.

A ripple of excitement spread as the daylight began to shift. People tilted their heads to watch the slow encroachment of Lunaterra's shadow on the moon. Conversations hushed, replaced by a collective breath of awe. I slipped out of the vibrant scene, my steps purposeful as they carried me toward the prison.

The moment I crossed the threshold into the prison, the air shifted. It reeked of mildew, unwashed bodies, and the sharp tang of despair. The weak flicker of torchlight cast jagged shadows on the damp stone walls, their surfaces streaked with grime and moisture.

The lively sounds of the impending eclipse and wedding festivities faded into muffled echoes, replaced by the harsh scrape of metal against stone, the rattling of chains, and the occasional low groan from a prisoner buried deep in their misery. A chill seeped into my skin, biting through the coarse fabric of the dress I'd borrowed from Charlotte to disguise myself. Though borrow was the wrong word. I knew she wouldn't want this back.

My fingers tightened around the pardon papers I held. My fingertips whitened as the weight of what I was doing pressed down on me like the cold, damp air around me. I set the papers inside a window, my knuckles cracked as I coaxed my fingers to release their hold.

"Pardon papers."

The guard's thick fingers unfolded the papers I presented him, his brow furrowing as he scanned the page. The prince's seal glinted in the dim torchlight. I held my breath, praying I'd done it right. I'd taken the seal from Adom's desk after climbing out of his bed last night.

With a grunt, the guard retrieved a heavy ring of keys from his belt. "Follow me."

He led me down a dim corridor, the keyring at his side jingling with each heavy step. The walk likely took five minutes, but it felt like hours. Finally, we arrived at a cell in the darkest part of the prison. The figure inside was just a shadow slumped in the far corner, motionless. The guard unlocked the iron bars with a grunt and swung the door open.

"He's all yours."

Jorge emerged, his gait uneven, and it was only then I realized why. He favored one side, the side where he was armless. Stripped of the technology that made him a formidable warrior, he looked smaller somehow. Vulnerable. But his glare—sharp and unyielding—held no weakness.

His eyes landed on me, and I felt their weight immediately. He knew. He knew I wasn't Charlotte. The silence was crushing, but I didn't break it. Instead, I stepped forward, my arm outstretched to help steady him.

He recoiled from my touch, jerking back as though I was about to gut him. I couldn't blame him. The lies, the betrayals—they were a knot so tangled I couldn't tell who was the most guilty. Him, Charlotte, Adom… or me. All I knew was that none of us would escape this unscathed.

The walk to the prison doors felt endless. Neither of us spoke. When we reached the entrance, the guard handed Jorge his prosthetics, piece by piece. The gates clanged shut with the two of us on the other side.

Outside, the Hunter's Moon dominated the sky. Avarix's once-bright surface was nearly consumed by Lunaterra's shadow. A deep, coppery hue spread across his face, the pale silver glow replaced by a haunting red. The air felt heavier, as if the eclipse had drawn the breath from the heavens.

Jorge sat on a raised stone and began to put himself back together. I stood back, silent, as he methodically reattached his prosthetics. There was something ritual-istic about the way he secured the straps, tested the joints, and flexed his mechanical fingers. With each addition, the man who emerged from the cell became the warrior again, piece by piece, until he was whole—or as whole as he could be.

"Let me guess. She traded herself for my freedom."

I nodded, unable to meet his gaze.

"And you agreed because you love him."

I turned away, my throat tightening. Words wouldn't come.

"Yeah, I understand." Jorge gave a humorless laugh. "I had every plan to kill that bastard, but he got under my skin, too."

The breath I'd been holding slipped out, half a laugh, half a sigh. "Adom acts like he's a monster. But he's really just a cub who wants to cuddle."

Jorge actually gave an amused laugh this time. "I'm sure he'll appreciate hearing that from the woman he loves."

I glanced at him, surprised, and found his grin mirrored my own. Two strangers bound by a shared burden. It was a fleeting connection, but one I desperately needed.

Then the wedding bells tolled.

The actual vow part of Lunaterran weddings was the fastest part of the rituals. It would all be over in ten minutes. There was no way we could make it to the palace in time to stop it. Even if that had been a thought in Jorge's mind, he didn't move from the rock. I sank down beside him.

Ten minutes passed. I doubt either of us breathed once during that time.

Something would go wrong. Adom would realize the fairy he was marrying wasn't me, and he'd call it off. Charlotte would get cold feet and run away again.

The wedding bells tolled a second time, announcing that the vows had been said. It was done. Adom and Charlotte were married.

In silent agreement, Jorge and I shifted our weight on the rock to move to standing. We rose on unsteady feet and looked around us. Overhead, the shadow of Lunaterra was fully seated over Avarix. The First Moon had a red tinge across its face, as though it had been scarred. I don't know about Jorge, but I certainly felt like a blood sacrifice.

And then a roar shook the ground.

It rolled through the city like thunder, raw and guttural, resonating with primal power. It wasn't a roar of celebration or triumph. It was rage—and heartbreak.

Jorge and I shared another look. This one was filled with the smallest hint of hope. Before we could move, we were surrounded. Guards poured in from every direction. Not shifter guards. These were fae. Jorge's body tensed beside me, his mechanical limbs whirring faintly as he prepared to fight.

CHAPTER EIGHTEEN

ADOM

The weight of the moment pressed against my chest. Not in a suffocating way. I was acutely aware of every breath in my lungs, every beat of my heart. It was finally here. My wedding day.

The day I'd dreaded all my life, a fate I'd once resented, now had my heart racing in anticipation.

All eyes were on me as I entered the throne room. They weren't fixed on my claws or the unnatural strength in my steps. Instead, they followed the lines of the wedding suit Charlotte had tailored for me, to me. The fabric fit my frame so precisely that it felt like a second skin. The deep hues and intricate embroidery caught the light with every movement.

Perhaps Charlotte had been right—maybe it wasn't my beastly features that had appalled the kingdom all these years. Maybe it had been the clothes I'd worn without care, more armor than attire.

Not that the court's opinions mattered much to me. All that mattered to me was the woman waiting at the end of this path. The woman I was going to spend the rest of my life with, starting now.

The Lioness Queen sat poised on her throne. This was the last day she would sit there, the final hours before the weight of the crown shifted entirely to me. Once I took a bride, my mother would become the dowager queen, stepping back from her reign to make way for my and Charlotte's rule.

Queen Amara had given much to the crown. She had lost the other part of her soul, the man she had loved more than life itself. If I lost Charlotte… I swallowed hard. If I lost her, I would fall into the same darkness my mother had. I would never come out.

The Lioness' gaze landed on me. I braced myself for the flinch. It didn't come.

Those amber eyes, so like my own, held no emotion, no warmth. They were calm pools of nothingness. I was used to this expression, or lack thereof, and yet it still unsettled me in some small way, a reminder of the chasm that had always existed between us even when my father was alive.

The great doors creaked open, the sound echoing in the cavernous room. The herald announced the bride's arrival. My mother's expression didn't falter at first—but when Charlotte stepped into the room, a ripple broke through her mask. She flinched.

It was slight, barely noticeable. To me, it might as well have been an earthquake. My mother's hand tightened on the lion's head carved into the arm of the throne. It wasn't like her to let anything show, to give anyone the satisfaction of knowing she felt anything at all.

I turned away from my mother. The best man's spot stood vacant, a silent reminder of Jorge's betrayal. I clenched my jaw and pushed the thought aside. This wasn't the time for anger, for hurt. Not when I had the one person who would never betray me walking toward me.

Charlotte was a vision, a dream, draped in sunshine yellow that clung to her figure and shimmered in the candlelight. The gown was perfection, every detail meticulously crafted. The veil covered her face again. I kept in the laugh but couldn't hide my smirk at its return. I couldn't wait to lift it, to see her eyes and kiss her mouth, to claim her as mine forever.

As she drew closer, a strange unease settled in the

pit of my stomach. It was subtle, like a whisper just out of hearing distance, a sense that something was… off. Her walk, her posture—there was a stiffness, a restraint that I couldn't quite place.

The veil was different. Likely because the one she'd worn back at the Summer Castle had been damaged or dirty or perhaps left behind as we'd fled the troll attack. The veil didn't matter. I'd seen all of her and accepted every part.

When she reached me, I stepped forward, taking her gloved hand in mine. Her hand was cool to the touch. Likely because of the chill of the room. Outside, an eclipse was happening. In the full light of day, the planet was moving between the suns and the moon, casting Avarix into darkness.

"Under the gaze of Lyra, our steadfast Daughter Sun, and in the shadow of Avarix, the First Moon in his eternal pursuit, we gather to witness the binding of two souls. Let the vows spoken here today ripple across the stars, uniting not just two lives but two destinies."

The officiant turned to Charlotte, inviting her to begin.

"Adom…" Her voice trembled as though she'd never spoken my name before. "Like the moons that chase the sun through endless skies, you have pursued me. In finding each other, we have ended the chase. You, my moon, are my constant, the one who draws my light and protects me in the darkness. Together, we will illuminate what lies ahead, guiding each other through every phase and every cycle. With our paths aligned, may our combined light please the gods."

"Your Highness," prompted the officiant.

I could hardly breathe, let alone speak, as my love's words settled over me. I swore I felt the curse lifting from my chest with her promises. When my words came, they spilled from the depths of my soul.

"Charlotte, like the moons that chase the sun through endless skies, I have pursued you. In finding each other, we have ended the chase. You, my sun, are my guiding light, the one who gives purpose to my orbit and fills my shadows with warmth. Without you, I am a mere reflection; with you, I shine. I vow to follow you through every sky, to protect you when darkness falls, and to embrace your light until the stars fade and the heavens are no more. With our paths aligned, may our combined light please the gods."

Her lips parted slightly. Through the veil, I could see the emotion pooling in her eyes. They sparkled like pools of blue.

The officiant spoke again, inviting us to join hands. I took hers fully, wrapping them in mine. Her fingertips were ragged, the skin was torn. Had she been up all night reworking her dress? No, she had been riding me. Her fingers had been soft at my cock.

"May your union burn bright, may your light shine on each other, and may you find balance in each other's orbit for the rest of your days. You may now kiss your bride."

I lifted her veil. Slowly, since I was unveiling the most precious treasure. Her beauty struck me like a meteor shower, sudden and brilliant, leaving an imprint I would never forget. But it felt like I was seeing her for the first time.

Her lips did not form the smile she always gifted me. They formed a single word.

"Sorry."

She looked at me with sad blue eyes. She held my hand with the callused fingers of a warrior. I didn't feel the pull to her that I had from the first moment she walked into the room at the Summer Castle.

This was not her. This was not my *little sphinx.*

"Kiss her, Adom." My mother's roar was quiet. She hadn't raised her voice since losing my father.

This woman who wasn't mine held still. I got the sense that that was unnatural for her. She appeared a ball of fury contained. Had she done something to my Charlotte?

"Do your duty, Adom."

I don't know how, but I knew that this was the princess I was destined to marry. She had the same wariness in her eyes that confronted me anytime I dared glance in a mirror. It was a look my *little sphinx* had never once bestowed upon me. She'd always looked at me in surprised delight, like she couldn't believe she was standing next to me.

"Where is she?" I didn't ask the imposter.

My mother pressed her lips together. She didn't flinch. She closed her eyes.

I opened my mouth to ask—no, to demand to know where the other half of my heart was. But human language escaped me. The roar that tore out of me was dark and twisted and filled with pain. Pain and magic. Magic and darkness. Darkness and light.

The light suffocated me. It filled every pore of my body until it was ripping me apart. The tearing happened with a ferocity that left me gasping. A vise unclamped from my ribs and broke open something caged deep within. The departure crushed me from the inside out. The absence was a void, a weightless, crushing hollowness that pressed down harder than the curse ever had.

My body trembled. My hands shook. My vision blurred. My head pounded. My pulse was a wild drumbeat in my ears, louder than my fading cries.

And then everything went black.

CHAPTER NINETEEN

BELLE

The nightmare was a single, unending roar of pain. It vibrated through my chest, like it was trying to pull me apart. I knew it was Adom. He was roaring in pain, in turmoil… and there was nothing I could do to stop the hurt.

My feet struggled to move. They sank into a sticky, invisible substance that clung to my shins like honey. I reached out, desperate to get to him. My upper body was swaddled in fabric—yards and yards of it, tangled around my arms, my legs, my throat.

I clawed at it, panic rising with every breath. It

smelled of roses, damp earth, and something faintly metallic—blood, maybe?

Finally, I broke free and opened my eyes to complete and total darkness.

It wasn't the comfortable dark of a room lit by wayward strands of moonlight. This was oppressive, heavy, like every source of light in the world had been swallowed whole. The air was too still, too quiet. I pushed myself upright, trying to get my bearings. Then realized I knew exactly where I was.

There was the small table where I'd set my tools as I'd sewn the threads of Adom's hair into the wedding gown. Curtains fluttered against the open window that Jorge had climbed in. Beyond the window was the faint outline of the woods where the trolls had emerged. I was back in the summer castle.

The door to the bedroom creaked open. It wasn't the whiff of flowers that I suspected that would herald the Fairy Queen's forest magic. It was the scent of savanna, a place I'd never been. But as the descendant of spring flowers, I knew my climates.

I smelled the sharpness of wind-carried dust and the faint memory of distant rain. Beneath it lingered the wild, untamed expanse of endless horizons where predators prowled and prey scattered like petals on the wind. The room shrank, shadows growing longer as the presence of the Lioness Queen filled it, commanding every inch of space without a single word.

My first thought was not for my safety or continued existence on this planet. "Is he okay?"

That roar had been guttural. It had sounded like he was dying. I needed to go to him, to hold him, to hug him, to kiss away any hurt and take it into myself. I wasn't a warrior. I couldn't fight. But I could soothe him.

"He's married."

Ouch. That stung. The queen and I were the same size. But one of us had delicate wings, and the other had teeth and claws.

"When did you know? That I wasn't her?"

"The moment I saw you look at him." Her golden eyes, so much like Adom's, glinted faintly in the darkness. They lacked the warmth his carried. Hers were—not lifeless. Just resigned. Like she'd given up on life.

I was beginning to understand the feeling. "Does he know?"

It was a stupid question. I regretted it the moment the words passed my lips. I knew the answer, but the queen let the words hang in the air like a seam frayed beyond repair.

"He knows."

Of course, he knew. Adom knew me. He *knew* me. He had studied me with those golden eyes that saw everything, even the parts of myself I'd tried to hide. It would be clear to him on first glance that Charlotte and I might favor, but we were nothing alike.

I was lace and silk, soft lines and delicate beading. She was unpolished leather, strong lines, and smudged ink.

Where I loved beauty, crafting it with needle and thread, Charlotte cared little for appearances. Dirt and sweat never fazed her. Rebellion and nonconformity oozed from her very pores. My fingertips had calluses from hours spent stitching; hers bore the marks of climbing, lifting, and wielding strength no one expected from a highborn fae.

The fairy princess could wrap herself in silence, using it as armor. She was secretive and held her confidences tightly to her chest. Words spilled out of me like ribbons unraveling from a spool.

Charlotte was the real deal. I'd only been pretending.

She didn't want the crown. Neither did I. I just wanted the prince.

"Adom's—His Royal Highness's curse is broken?"

"It's His Majesty. And not yet. But it will be. Once he and his wife complete the marriage ritual. They've said their vows. He need only kiss and bed her."

I tried to swallow, but there was something caught in my throat. It was my heart. I didn't fool myself into telling myself I didn't care. That was a lie. I did care. I cared about Adom getting the thing he wanted most in this world: freedom from that curse.

So I nodded to the queen.

The corner of her eyes lifted, like she recognized something in me. Perhaps her own reflection.

"Am I a prisoner here?"

"Prisoner? You, my dear, are the talk of the capital. The wedding dress you made for Queen Charlotte and the tailoring you did on my son's suit—Colson has been recording the names of the highborn and royal houses who want your business."

The words should have sparked elation. This was what I'd wanted, wasn't it? For my talent to be recognized, for my name to be spoken in drawing rooms and recognized in ballrooms. I'd imagined this moment countless times in Evergrove, when I'd stitched through the night until my fingers bled and my head hurt from dreams too big for my small world.

But all I could think about was Adom. His golden eyes, fierce and longing. The way he'd looked at me right before he kissed me. The raw tenderness in his voice when he said my name. Yes, he'd said her name, but he'd meant me. His little sphinx.

Charlotte wouldn't stay. She would run again. She'd leave Adom alone. Alone with a mother who would steal away his happiness all in the name of duty.

I couldn't bear the thought of him suffering, of the light in his eyes dimming under the weight of betrayal. All I wanted now was to make him happy, to stay by his side, even if it meant remaining in the shadows as nothing more than a servant. I didn't need to be his queen. I just wanted to be… his.

"You have choices." The Lioness Queen moved closer, her fingers brushing against a vial hanging from a chain around her neck. It was small, delicate, filled with a shimmering liquid that caught the faintest glimmers of light. "You can stay here, in the capital. Become the famed dressmaker you've always dreamed of. But you'll see them every day—King Adom and Queen Charlotte. Together. Not happy. Duty-bound.

"Or you can leave. Find a quiet life in another land and make your dresses. The hellhounds were quite impressed with your work."

Those really weren't choices. Stay and have a career while nursing a broken heart. Or leave and… what? My mind blanked at a world without Adom. My gaze went to the window. A sliver of sunlight returned to the moon, giving Avarix back his pale white glow.

"Where's Jorge?"

"The soldier? He's made his choice."

And so had I.

CHAPTER TWENTY

ADOM

*W*ill *they never learn, Mother?*

I keep trying to tell them, my little spark. But I fear my rays don't reach that far any longer.

This one listened.

I'd never been one for dreams. Not even as a child. I heard all that was around me from the time I was in the womb. When I closed my eyes each night, I tried to shut the world out. I often succeeded.

Except for now.

In the dream, I felt the sun on my skin—not on fur, but on skin. I lifted my hand, shielding my eyes. My fingers filtered the light, and from the shade of my palm I saw smooth, clawless digits. First five of them. Then five more joined them as I raised my other hand.

I like that he fights for her.

You like that he defied Him.

There was giggling in my head. The light shimmered in time to the sound. The twin stars in the sky twinkled. No, not twins. One was brighter than the other. Just like the mother and daughter suns of Lunaterra.

You're all fixed now, fierce cat.

Fixed? I looked at my hands again. Then down at the rest of me. I was naked inside my mind. No fur in sight. My skin was a light brown, darker than my father's golden tan and lighter than my mother's earth-brown.

The curse. The curse was gone.

And so was my *little sphinx*. The skies started to dim. The suns began to set.

"Wait. Wait! Take it back."

The suns didn't pause in their descent.

She was right to let you catch her, fierce cat. If only the others would learn from you.

And with that, the brightest sun dipped below the horizon. Only the faint glow of the larger sun remained, but Solara was descending fast.

They want to capture my daughter's light. But my bright little spark has no interest in being caught.

"I'll keep the curse. I'll give up my kingdom. Just let me keep her."

Solara didn't answer. I tried to keep my eyes shut. Tried to stay in the dream to reason with the goddesses. But the sunrays on my face were too bright. They forced my eyes open.

The room was dim, the curtains drawn, but enough light filtered in to confirm what I'd already suspected. My body felt different—lighter, unburdened. I lifted my hands. No claws. Just hands. My skin was smooth, unmarred, the color of milk swirled into a rich coffee. I ran my hands over my face, feeling the contours of a jaw, a nose, lips—human features.

I was whole. But that wasn't true. I was only half a man—if I was even that much without her.

I staggered to my feet. With no claws to anchor into the wood, I almost tripped over them in my haste. A mirror stood across the room. I stared into it, hardly believing the image before me.

My hair was still wild, a mane of gold, bronze, and brown. It framed the face of a clean-shaven man. I traced the reflection with my fingers, still not quite fully believing my eyes.

The curse was broken.

A throat cleared behind me. I turned, expecting to see her, my lavender beauty, my *little sphinx*.

The woman who sat by the door wasn't her. She was lavender-skinned, yes, but her eyes were a shade of cool blue, not verdant green. Her hair was an untidy mess, as though she'd struggled recently. She was dressed in a wedding gown—*her* wedding gown. But that wasn't the most interesting thing about her.

She toyed with a dagger, flipping it over her palm and between her fingers as she regarded me. The dagger was beautiful. Sharp with the dark, rusty red of blood along the edge.

"Hi. I'm Charlotte. Your wife."

"I'm Adom. Your husband."

We awkwardly eyed each other. I sat heavily on the bed, running a hand through my wild mane. Charlotte hesitated, then joined me, her posture rigid as she sat down.

"Are you planning to use that?"

"It's beautiful, isn't it? Jorge made it for me for my twelfth birthday."

Jorge. The pieces were slowly putting themselves together in my mind. "He was planning to rescue you. Not her."

Charlotte—this Charlotte, not my Charlotte, nodded.

"Where is she?"

"I don't know."

I rose from the bed and stalked to the door. It was locked. I didn't even know my bedroom door could lock. I'd never had occasion to do so.

"We're under orders from the Skykeeper Mages to finish the marriage ritual before they'll let us out."

"Finish?"

"You know…" She motioned to the ruffled sheets where I'd slept alone dreaming of the two suns. "I didn't touch you while you were sleeping. Even though my consent was taken from me on the day I was born, I wasn't going to take yours from you."

"But you were going to give yourself to me, to this union?"

"No." She flipped the dagger again. "I wasn't planning to stay long."

"Jorge is waiting for you somewhere?"

She cocked her head, narrowing those blue eyes at me. "You didn't have him taken?"

"I have no idea where he went after he tried to steal her." I didn't even know her name.

The real Princess Charlotte began to pace. Though I suppose now that we were married, she was Queen Charlotte. "Then she must have him."

"Who?"

"She'll kill him this time." Charlotte kicked at the door. It shuddered but didn't budge open. She turned to me, her eyes wild. "If she has Jorge, she'll have Belle too."

"Who's..." But I knew who Belle was. The name suited her: round and soft.

"I ran from you at the Summer Castle, and Belle was forced by my mother to take my place. Belle and I traded places last night. She went to save Jorge in exchange for me taking my place and marrying you so that I could break the curse."

Her explanation was dizzying, but I caught on. A low rumble started in my chest. The lion who was a part of me had just woken up to find itself caged inside a man's body.

"Belle wanted to marry you. I think she actually loves you. But she knew she couldn't break the curse. And I had to save Jorge. I love him with all of my heart, and I won't let her take him away from me again. He's mine."

I had been born a curse, a sacrifice to a bitter god. Belle had sacrificed herself for me. No one had ever done that for me.

Outside, the moon was still cloaked in the planet's shadow. Avarix was held in check. Was the curse truly broken? Or was this just a cruel temporary reprieve? It didn't matter. Curse or no curse, I would get Belle back.

My foot lashed out and into the heavy door. The

impact sent a jolt through my body and through the door. It shuddered but didn't come off its frame.

Of course it didn't. These were the king's rooms. Reinforced, designed to withstand sieges, invasions, and now, apparently, a man desperate to get to the one person who mattered. If I still had the strength of my lion, I could have torn it down in one blow. But the lion was trapped, caged inside me.

I was fixed now, they'd said. I wouldn't be fixed until she was back in my arms. A roar ripped from my throat as the beast clawed to get out.

And then I remembered; I was fixed. No longer trapped between two worlds. I was fixed. I was whole.

I'd seen shifters change forms every day of my life. I'd felt the envy in my gut. Every day, I'd wanted to shift fully into a man. For my very first change, I shifted fully into the other part of me. With one more blow that came from my two front paws, the door came crashing to the ground.

CHAPTER TWENTY-ONE

BELLE

The last rays of the setting sun kissed the horizon as I clawed my way out of the bedroom window. The lunar eclipse was nearly over. Avarix shed the shadow of Lunaterra inch by inch, leaving behind a haunting crescent shape. His silvery light bathed the vines I clung to, glinting off the dewdrops and turning them into tiny jewels.

There was nothing beautiful about this moment. Not the chill of the air against my torn dress. Not the sting of fresh cuts on my palms. Certainly not the burning ache in my arms as I fought to climb down.

How had Jorge managed to climb up? How had Adom followed him up so quickly that night? Even Charlotte had done this at the Pridehaven Palace. Clearly, I was the weak link in this merry band.

I had thought going down would be easier than going up, but every slip of my foot, every crack of a branch beneath my weight sent my heart lurching. I wasn't a warrior. I wasn't brave or strong. But I was going to fight to get back to Adom, even if it killed me.

When my feet hit the ground, my knees buckled. I collapsed into the dirt, gasping for air. My fingers were bloody and trembling. My dress was little more than shredded fabric hanging from my shoulders. Mud streaked my arms and legs.

The forest loomed dark and endless. The trees swayed in a gentle breeze that did nothing to calm the rising storm of my fear. How was I going to make it back to the capital on my own?

The queen had said I wasn't a captive, but I seriously doubted she'd give me a ride. And the door to the room had been locked. I'd checked.

I forced myself to take the first step. My shoes sank into the damp earth as I stumbled toward the trees. Every nerve in my body screamed at me to turn back, to stop this madness. But I couldn't. Not now. Not ever.

Every rustle of leaves and chirp of insects was a dagger of sound that set my pulse racing. A branch snapped somewhere to my left. I whirled, my breath catching in my throat.

Nothing. It was nothing. Just my mind playing tricks on me. Hopefully.

A roar shattered the stillness, primal and bone-deep. My heart seized as I turned toward the sound. It had to be her. The Lioness Queen. She'd come for me, and this time, she wouldn't leave anything to chance.

But then I saw it—a flash of golden and bronze mane rippling in the moonlight like liquid fire. My heart stopped. Then it soared. It wasn't the Lioness Queen.

It was Adom. He'd come for me. He'd found me.

His massive form moved through the trees with a predator's grace, each bound shaking the earth. His impossibly large paws hit the earth with a muted thunder, claws glinting faintly as they sank into the soil. His chest as a lion was just as broad as his chest as a man. Muscles rippled beneath a sleek coat of golden fur. His tail lashed behind him, long and sinuous, a whip of control and fury. His familiar eyes locked on to me; the possessive glint in them made me stop in my tracks.

The joy twisted into something darker as my gaze fell to the figure riding his back. Charlotte. In my wedding dress.

Her dagger gleamed in her hand. Her eyes burned with a fire I'd never seen before. She let out a bloodcurdling war cry and hurled the blade with deadly precision.

The world slowed, my thoughts spinning wildly. Were they together now? A unit, their union cemented by the breaking of the curse? Had Adom betrayed me, too? My breath hitched as I watched the dagger fly, its silver edge glinting like the crescent moon above. Was this how it would end?

But the blade sailed past me, the wind of its passage brushing against my cheek and lodged with a sickening thud into the skull of a fae soldier I hadn't seen—or heard—approaching from behind. The man crumpled to the ground with his sword in his hand.

I stood frozen, staring at the body, then at Charlotte, whose eyes burned not with hatred but with determination. I swallowed the breath I'd been holding. Then panted in sharp, ragged bursts as realization crashed over me.

They weren't here to kill me.

They'd come to save me.

The arms that came around me were warm, firm … and entirely unfamiliar. I stiffened, turning sharply to see who held me. He was a stranger. Likely another enemy soldier.

I screamed for Adom. Where was he? My fist flew instinctively, catching the man square in the nose.

He winced but didn't let go, his hand brushing over

his face as he gave me a familiar, disapproving scowl. That scowl. I knew that scowl.

"Adom?"

He stood bare, his bronzed skin catching the pale light of the moon, now fully free from Lunaterra's shadow. This was no beast. This was Adom, fully human.

"What did I tell you?" He roared the words. The trees shuddered with the force of the sound as he backed me into the bark of an ancient oak. "I told you not to run, little sphinx. I told you that I have your scent inside me. I told you I'd catch you if you ran from me."'

"I had to go. If I didn't, you would still be cursed."

"What did you tell me?"

The bark of the tree dug into my back as he loomed over me. This time, he didn't give me the answers. He waited for me to respond. I knew what he wanted me to say.

"I told you that I loved you."

"Wrong tense." His growl shook the branches above us and the ground beneath my feet.

"I love you, Adom."

"You said you didn't care what I looked like."

"And I meant it. But it mattered to *you*. I just wanted you to have what you wanted. I wanted you to be happy."

"You are the only thing in this world that makes me happy."

He pressed his lips to mine in a kiss that reasserted his claim on my heart. There was still a bite to it. He growled as he licked into my mouth. When he broke the kiss, I looked into his clean-shaven face, devoid of fur or sharp teeth. He still looked fierce and untamed, but he wasn't yet familiar to me as the Beast Prince had been.

"You… you did it. You broke the curse." The words came out hollow, void of the joy I should've felt. My heart twisted, caught in the tangled threads of heartbreak and hope.

If the curse was broken, it meant only one thing—Adom and Charlotte had completed their vows.

"I didn't break it. We broke it. Together."

"You don't have to get graphic about it, Adom."

His hands settled on my arms. I wanted to yank away from his furless touch. But I held still. This was what the Lioness Queen had warned me about. It didn't matter. I wasn't leaving him. Because I knew sooner or later Charlotte would.

"Belle." It was the first time he'd said my name. It slipped from his lips like a prayer. "You and I broke the curse."

"I don't understand."

"I gave you my vows, as you did to me. I gave you

my body, as you gave yours to me. Then the suns showed mercy."

The world stilled as I fought to catch up. Everything around me, inside me, was spinning. When it all righted, I knew three things. The curse was broken. Adom was whole. And we could be together. It was all that mattered to me.

I surged forward, my hands tangling in his hair as my lips found his. This kiss was desperate, filled with every unspoken word and longing I couldn't put into speech. His arms wrapped around me, pulling me closer until there was no space left between us.

A throat cleared somewhere behind us. We broke apart to see Charlotte standing with a bloodied dagger in her hand, wearing the torn wedding dress.

"Where's Jorge?"

CHAPTER TWENTY-TWO

ADOM

The cool air of the Summer Castle kissed my bare skin as Belle and I stepped through its towering front doors. My hand engulfed hers, our fingers laced tightly. I knew letting go wouldn't mean losing her again, but I'd used up my quota of rational until the next Hunter's Eclipse.

No one batted an eyelash at my nudity. Well, that wasn't entirely true. I caught a couple of female guards blinking a little too fast, their eyes darting down before snapping back up. One of the men's eyes lingered a second too long, and I arched a brow at him until he cleared his throat and looked away.

"Your Majesty." Colson appeared, holding a dark robe in his hands.

I took the robe, shrugging it over my shoulders. Would I ever get used to fabric directly on my flesh? As soon as I'd tied the sash, I reached for Belle again, retaking her hand.

The sitting room came into view. My mother sat in the same chair where I'd first seen Belle. The memory of that moment was vivid—her needle weaving my hair into the threads of her wedding dress. The dress she'd made for someone else, while my heart had already begun to beat for her.

Through the window, the First Moon hovered low in the sky. Its pale white face was marred by faint red shadows left behind by Lyra's rays from the eclipse. Those would fade in a day. For now, it appeared Avarix glowered at me.

I stared the moon down, unflinching. Avarix could rage all he wanted. He would not retaliate. Not with Lyra's favor firmly on my side. We were safe now—Belle, my people, all of us.

Turning my gaze back to the room, I focused on my mother. Her expression was as neutral as ever, her face devoid of the warmth I'd long given up hoping to find.

Her sharp eyes flicked briefly to Belle and then back to me, taking in every detail.

Her lips pressed into a thin line. Her fingers curled slightly over the armrests of her chair. Whatever game she intended to play, I wasn't going to let her win. Not this time.

The moonlight from the window brushed over her face, but it didn't soften her. It had always been this way. From my earliest memory, she had looked at me with that same stoic mask. As though every glance burned her, but she refused to turn away. She turned away from me now, her head down and her eyes closed firmly shut.

"Can you not even look at me now, Mother? Now that I'm cured?"

"You look like your father."

That gave me pause. It was both compliment and slap to the heart. "And now you hate me for that, too."

She lifted her head and looked at me in confusion. "Hate you?"

"Because I'm the reason he's dead."

"No, Adom. I'm the reason he's dead. I'm the reason for all of this. I fell in love. I followed my heart when I should have obeyed the gods. And you—" Her voice faltered, but she pushed on. "You paid the price for my selfishness. Your father paid the price. Our people paid it in blood. Do you know what it's like to watch your child suffer and know it's your fault? To know the gods marked you for ruin because you dared to defy them?"

"I don't blame you for anything. I never have. I was proud to have been born of my father's love and your strength. Did you ever consider that Solara blessed you with Father? You had ten years with him. Your child was born healthy, if not whole."

My mother's gaze hardened again. "I thought if I showed you love, the moon would punish you more. Avarix is a jealous god. He would have taken everything from you, from us. He still might. That's why you must give her up. If you don't, the moon will destroy you and this kingdom."

"Fuck the moon."

It came out as a growl, low and menacing, like the beast that I was at my core. For the first time in my life, I saw fear in her eyes.

"I no longer serve Avarix. I no longer bow to his will. I gave my vows to Belle. I gave her my body, my soul. She broke the curse. Not Charlotte. Belle is queen."

The cool mask of the Lioness Queen was back in place. I don't know if she agreed with me, pitied me, or would defy me. One never knew with her.

Her gaze moved to Belle, standing silent and strong beside me. Something fragile flickered in my mother's eyes. Her fingers moved to the vial around her neck. I had always figured she was waiting for this day, the day I took the crown from her, to take the poison.

My mother tugged on the chain. There was a snap in the silence of the room. The chain broke, and the vial came to rest in the palm of her hand.

I tensed, unsure if I would snatch it from her hands before a drop hit her tongue. Or if I'd let her go to my father, which I knew was her heart's desire. Instead of uncorking the vial, my mother set it down on the table with a deliberate clink.

"Belle? Is that your name, child?"

Belle started beside me, then cleared her throat. "Yes, Your Majesty."

"We have much to do if you are to rule by his side. Table manners and dining etiquette at dawn. If I must spend the rest of my days taming a wildflower into a garden rose, so be it."

Then, without another word, she rose and left, her steps measured, her head held high. A lioness to the end.

CHAPTER TWENTY-THREE

BELLE

The door to the castle's bedroom clicked shut, leaving me alone with him at last. We'd decided to stay a few days at the Summer Castle to have a proper honeymoon. Though it was mostly the nights I was interested in.

Adom turned to me, his golden eyes fierce, soft, and everything in between. He reached for me. His large hands cradled my face. He looked down at me in the way that had made my heart first skip a beat.

How could I have doubted he'd mistake me for

Charlotte? How could I have believed he would remain duty bound to her? Not when that spark in his eyes told me I was his world.

His lips hovered close, so close to mine. I wanted to fall into the moment, into him. But something wasn't quite right.

"What's wrong?" Of course, he'd sense something was off. He paid as much attention to me as I paid to my stitching.

I managed a small, apologetic smile, even as my heart pounded. There was an unspoken pact between us. We were going to be completely honest with each other from now on.

"I'm sorry... I'm just still getting used to this—this version of you."

His hands lowered from my face. His head dipped to look down between us at the robe that was already coming undone. He was completely hairless. No fur in sight, even on his chest. Had I developed a fur fetish?

"A fur fetish?" he asked.

Had I said that out loud? By the look of his quizzically raised brow, I had.

"Do you not like the way that I look?"

"You look great. Handsome. Strong. Smooth." I was running out of descriptors. "It's not that I don't... find you attractive in your skin. It's just...I just... miss the fur."

"You miss the fur?"

"Am I perverted for finding you sexier as a beast?"

For a heartbeat, there was only silence. Then he laughed—a deep, rumbling sound that sent a delicious shudder across my shoulder blades.

Adom tilted his forehead against mine, his closeness grounding me. "You can have me any way you want me, little sphinx."

He tore the robe off. The man really was well made. Every line and muscle carved as though Solara had fashioned him from a blazing star. His broad, powerful shoulders gave way to a chest that rose and fell with steady, self-assured confidence. His bronze skin bore faint scars from battles fought and survived. Each ridge of his abdomen spoke of endurance and perseverance. Then the air around him began to shift.

The transformation was slow, deliberate. It was like watching raw power in motion—the ripple of muscles, the elongation of his frame as his human features melted away. The sinewy muscles beneath his bronze skin rippled as dark fur spread across his chest. His face elongated, the sharpness of his jaw softening into a beastly muzzle. His claws extended, sleek and sharp. His mane—that wild, untamed cascade of bronze, gold, and brown—remained the same regal halo around his face.

"Adom."

I leaned closer, my nose brushing against his fur, and I felt his warmth seep into me. His deep rumble of contentment vibrated against my palm. This was him, the beast-man I had fallen in love with. I would take him any way I could get him. But I loved him in this form the most.

With a swipe of his claw, he cut the fabric of my torn gown. My wings came free. "When we're alone, do not hide these from me."

"You show me what I like. I'll show you what you like."

I fluttered my wings and got the exact response I'd been hoping for. His nose brushed the edge of my wing. He inhaled deeply. The sound of his breath was both a claim and a caress. Then he licked the tip and made my whole body clench.

"Can I fuck you now?"

"Yes, Your Majesty."

His lips curved into a wicked grin, his voice thick with authority. "On the bed."

Heat shot through me, but I didn't hesitate. I did as I was told. Just like any girl would who had common sense, knowing she was about to bang a beast.

Shadows flickered like a living audience to the moment unfolding between us. The bed beneath me was soft, its sheets a velvety cocoon that cradled my trembling body. Adom loomed above me, his beastly form a perfect blend of power and grace, his amber eyes glowing with hunger.

His clawed hands slid along my thighs, parting them with a tenderness that belied the raw energy radiating from him. I melted beneath his touch, gasping as his furred chest brushed against my bare skin.

His breath was hot against my neck. His lips grazed the sensitive curve where my shoulder met my wing. My fingers curled into the sheets as he pressed a kiss there, his sharp teeth teasing the edge of pain and pleasure.

"Adom…"

His massive hand slid between my thighs. The heat pooling there was making my entire body feverish. Adom's deep rumble of satisfaction vibrated through me when he found just how ready I was.

I felt the blunt heat of him press against my entrance. My body arched instinctively as he teased me, the head of his cock rubbing against my slick folds. He held himself there for a moment, his claws digging into the sheets on either side of me as he fought for control.

"Please, Adom."

That was all he needed. He thrust forward, his thick length stretching me in a single, powerful motion. I cried out. My wings sprang open like my core as he filled me completely, his massive body pinning me to the bed. The pleasure was overwhelming, a delicious ache that consumed every part of me.

His hips pulled back, only to surge forward again, harder, faster. Each thrust drove me higher. The intensity of his movements stole my breath. His claws dug into my hips, holding me in place as he took me with wild abandon, his growls mingling with my cries of pleasure.

The bed creaked beneath us. The rhythm of his thrusts shook the furniture. My wings flared wide, the sensation of the silken sheets against them amplifying the fire building within me. My nails raked across his back, drawing a roar from him that only spurred him on.

"Adom," I gasped, my voice breaking as the tension in my body coiled tighter, ready to snap. "I'm close…"

"Wait for me," he commanded, his voice feral.

His hips slammed into mine, each thrust driving me closer. I held on for dear life, waiting for him like I'd been told to do. The slight smirk on his face told me he was trying to hold out, trying to make it last. But our bodies had different plans.

I saw the moment he lost control. He grabbed my hand, wrapping his fingers with mine as we both leaped together. And then we shattered. My body convulsed around him as his climax crashed over me.

His release filled me in hot, pulsing waves. The force

of it left us both trembling. His massive body collapsed over mine as we sank into the bed, our breaths mingling in the heated air.

There was only the sound of our breathing. The faint hum of my fluttering wings as they slowly stilled. He lifted his head, his gaze softening as he looked at me, his beastly features utterly tender.

I gave him a self-satisfied smile. "Hey."

"Hmmm?" It was a more deep purr than a question.

"I think I'm gonna run from you again tomorrow."

"You won't get past the door."

"Yes. I think it's an excellent plan too."

He chuckled, reaching out an arm and pulling me into him. I came willingly, like I always would. He moved my hair from the nape of my neck. Glancing at me with a half-lidded gaze, he ran his tongue over his canine, then looked pointedly at my collarbone.

My breath hitched as I came to understand what he wanted. I gave him him nod. He was on me before my chin dipped to my chest.

His incisors pierced my skin, breaking flesh and finding the sap that was my life's blood. I expected pain from his bite, and there was some. But it was muted next to the overwhelming pleasure. My channel clenched as he pulled at the place he marked me. I pressed my thighs together but got no relief as my body vibrated from his claiming.

"You're mine now," he said, his voice a low, satisfied rumble.

My fingers tangled in the fur of his mane. "And you're mine."

We stayed like that, tangled in each other, the world, the suns and the moons beyond the room fading away.

EPILOGUE

JORGE

The shackles weighed heavily on my wrists, biting into the raw skin beneath. Every jolt of the carriage sent a fresh wave of pain up my arms and across my back. My body screamed in protest. I bit down on the agony. Pain was an old friend. It had walked beside me in the games, in the barracks, and now in the rattling dark of this cursed wagon.

The carriage ground to a halt, the wooden wheels creaking against the gravel road. My ears perked at the sound of another set of wheels coming to rest nearby. Through the small, barred window, I caught a glimpse of the royal crest embossed on a carriage gilded in gold. My stomach twisted as I prepared to face the nemesis that had somehow become one of my best friends. One of two friends I'd collected in my life.

I imagined Adom's claws around my throat as he stalked out of his carriage. I'd seen his rage on the battlefield. Now it would be directed at me and rightfully so. I had already proven that I would kill for her.

But when the door to the royal carriage swung open, it wasn't Adom who descended.

At the Lioness Queen's direction, the doors to my cage were opened. The guards reached in and dragged Belle's limp body from the carriage like a sack of flour. The sight of her—so small, so still—clenched something deep in my chest. She looked so much like Charlotte. Neither of them had done anything to deserve this.

"Take her inside," the Lioness Queen ordered. Her voice was low and steady, the kind of tone that brooked no argument. The guards obeyed without hesitation, carrying Belle into the Summer Castle as though the weight of her body didn't matter.

The Lioness turned, her golden eyes locking on me. I straightened as much as my bound frame would allow.

"You were his friend."

Oh, she thought I'd betrayed her son. I was honestly surprised to consider that she might care for Adom at having seen the utter lack of affection she'd showed him the years I knew him. "I am his friend."

"Yet you were going to steal his bride."

Going to steal his bride? Because Adom and Charlotte were married now. Not that it would stop me from finding my way back to her. I'd clawed and fought my way to stand at the Beast Prince's side because I knew that on this day, she would have to come and stand next to him. I'd find my way to her again. No matter where she was. No matter how long it took to reach her.

"She is my world. My heart is hers to command. As long as she wants me, I'll fight to get back to her."

The Lioness Queen's eyes narrowed, a flicker of something unreadable crossing her face. Before she could respond, another voice cut through the air like a hiss of venom.

"He won't be fighting much longer." The Fairy Queen appeared, her pale skin shimmering under the light of the two suns. Her eyes glinted with malice as she glared at me.

The Lioness Queen didn't acknowledge Queen Indira immediately. She kept her gaze fixed on me. "You would betray your future king, your country, for that fairy?"

"Didn't you do the same, Your Majesty, for a human?"

Her lips twitched in the ghost of a smile, but it didn't reach her eyes. "I did. And we all suffered for it." She finally turned to the Fairy Queen, her golden gaze like the sun itself. "It was a dangerous game you attempted to play. Attempted and lost. I pray she grants you a quick death. We should all be so lucky."

The Lioness Queen, disappeared and the Fairy Queen filled my view. This woman was the reason for my current condition: the loss of my hand, the three-year separation from Charlotte, and my current, though temporary, incarceration.

"I wish I could kill you now and be done with it, but I have to return to Evergrove. A mother's work is never done."

"You were never a mother to her. You were a madam."

Queen Indira snapped her fingers at the guards. "Make it slow." Her voice dripped with venom. "Make it agonizing. And leave the body for the trolls."

The carriage lurched forward again, this time taking flight. The pegasuses' wings beat heavily against the air, but I felt the uneven gait beneath us. Something was wrong. The carriage swayed unnaturally, the wheels clattering ever so often as if they scraped against an uneven track. We weren't going to get far, and when they landed, I'd be ready.

But ready for what? To go back to the capital and

save Charlotte? Was I really saving her? What would life with me even look like? What did I have to offer a fairy princess who was now queen?

Adom wasn't a bad man, far from it. He was one of the best men I knew. He wouldn't love her, but he would take care of her.

That was the issue. Charlotte needed love. Deserved it. She had withered under her mother's poisonous care until I'd shown up in her barn twelve years ago. I couldn't stand by and watch her live an unhappy life. It just wasn't in me. So I would have to break out.

*Read the breakout that happens in the near future,
the meeting in the barn that happened in the past,
and find out what's in store for the present for
Charlotte and Jorge in "Beautiful Blade."*

ABOUT INES JOHNSON

Lover of fairytales, folklore, and mythology, Ines Johnson spends her days reimagining the stories of old in a modern world. She writes books where damsels cause the distress, princesses wield swords, and moms save the world.

If you liked Ines' Beast then you'll love her Vampires and Dragons. To find out more just visit https://ineswrites.com/ReaderGroup

More PARANORMAL and FANTASY ROMANCE by INES JOHNSON

Dark Vintage

Her Vampire Prince

Her Vampire Lord

Her Vampire Knight

His Vampire Princess

The Last Dragons

The Dragon's Reluctant Sacrifice
The Dragon's Ambivalent Sacrifice
The Dragon's Willing Sacrifice
The Dragon's Rebellious Sacrifice
The Dragon's Compliant Sacrifice
The Dragon's Forbidden Sacrifice